D0296751

Ghost
Soldier

Ghost
Soldier

THERESA BRESLIN

DOUBLEDAY

GHOST SOLDIER
A DOUBLEDAY BOOK 978 0 857 53305 0

Published in Great Britain by Doubleday,
an imprint of Random House Children's Publishers UK
A Random House Group Company

This edition published 2014

1 3 5 7 9 10 8 6 4 2

Text copyright © Theresa Breslin, 2014
Illustration copyright © Kate Leiper, 2014

The Random House Group Limited supports the Forest Stewardship Council® (FSC®), the
leading international forest-certification organisation. Our books carrying the FSC label are printed
on FSC®-certified paper. FSC is the only forest-certification scheme supported by the leading
environmental organisations, including Greenpeace. Our paper procurement policy can be found at
www.randomhouse.co.uk/environment.

MIX
Paper from
responsible sources
FSC® C016897

Set in 12/23.5 pt Adobe Caslon by Falcon Oast Graphic Art Ltd.

RANDOM HOUSE CHILDREN'S PUBLISHERS UK,
61–63 Uxbridge Road, London W5 5SA

www.randomhousechildrens.co.uk
www.totallyrandombooks.co.uk
www.randomhouse.co.uk

Addresses for companies within The Random House Group Limited can be found at:
www.randomhouse.co.uk/offices.htm

THE RANDOM HOUSE GROUP Limited Reg. No. 954009

A CIP catalogue record for this book is available from the British Library.

This book is for Brogan,

who named the puppy Sandy

CHAPTER ONE

Guns firing.

Men yelling.

Smoke so thick that Rob can't see.

Another roar from the guns. The ground shudders. Stones and clods of earth rain down upon him. Rob stumbles, grabbing for something to hold.

Barbed wire.

Pain now. He looks at his hand, splashed with red. Blood. His blood . . . seeping between his fingers.

Help, he thinks. *I need help*. So he shouts. As loud as he can, he shouts: 'Help! Help!' But no sound comes out.

Rob puts his hands to his mouth. It's open. He *was*

shouting, but he isn't making any noise. He begins to panic, his heart thudding. He'll die here. Bleed to death in the smoke, and no one will know. Not his sister, Millie, nor his mum, nor his dad.

Dad.

It was Dad he'd come looking for. Dad who was lost in the war. And among the guns and the smoke, he, Rob, was trying to find him and bring him home.

But now they'll both be missing, far away in this strange land. Rob feels his body sag. He leans against the wall of the trench to rest. The smoke swirls, less dense than before. And there, through the fog of battle, a soldier is walking towards him.

'Dad!' Rob exclaims, reaching out his arms. The man in front of him does the same. 'Dad!' Rob calls again. 'I've been searching for you—' He stops.

The man facing him in the trench isn't wearing the uniform of the British Army. His clothes are the wrong colour. And on his head is a helmet with a spike at the top. This man is a German soldier!

The German raises his arms higher. In his hands he holds a gun. He points it at Rob.

Bang!

Rob feels a hard thump across his heart.

With a cry of terror he comes awake.

And he's lying in his bed at home with his dog sitting on his chest.

CHAPTER TWO

'Oh, Nell!'

Rob tried to push the dog off. But Nell was not to be moved. She licked his face as she always did each morning when she woke him.

Rob lay still for a minute to let his heart slow down. It was the second time this week he'd had a nightmare. The second awful dream since the telegram from the War Office arrived to say that his father was missing in action on the battlefields of the Western Front.

'Best dog in the world,' he whispered, stroking Nell's head. She gave a little yelp of happiness. 'Shhh!' Rob quietened her. 'We mustn't wake anyone else.'

He paused to hear if his mother was moving around downstairs, hoping that he hadn't disturbed her when shouting out in his sleep. But she was so upset by the arrival of the telegram about Dad that the local doctor had given her tablets to take at night, so now she slept later in the mornings.

'Quiet . . .' Rob spoke softly to his dog as he slid from the bed and pulled on his clothes. 'Remember the secret plan for today? We have to get past Millie's room without her knowing we're up.' Nell watched him with bright, intelligent eyes. 'She'd want to come along and that would hold us up and she'd get in the way.' Rob began to open his bedroom door. 'All right?' he asked, and utterly believed that his dog was nodding her head in complete understanding.

Boy and dog tiptoed onto the landing and down the rickety attic stairway to the ground floor of their farm cottage.

And there in the kitchen was Rob's little sister Millie, standing by the table spreading jam on thickly cut slices of bread.

'What are you doing?' he asked.

'Spreading plum jam on bread,' Millie answered, licking her sticky fingers.

'Why are you making plum-jam sandwiches at half past four in the morning?' Rob noticed that she was fully dressed and had her coat on.

''Cos plum jam is Dad's favourite,' said Millie. She replaced the lid on the jam jar. 'And when we find him he might be hungry, so I'm bringing these.' She put the sandwiches in a basket and covered them with a clean tea towel. 'There,' she said. 'I'm ready to go with you.'

'Where do you think I'm going?' Rob demanded.

'I don't know,' she replied. 'But last night I heard you telling Nell that you'd leave the kitchen window open so she could come in and wake you really early 'cos you were going to see if you could find Dad. And if you're going to run away to find Dad, I'm coming with you.'

'I'm not running away!' said Rob.

'Well, you're off out somewhere,' said Millie. 'You were saying to Nell how it was important to be up early this morning 'cos you had a plan to find Dad. Whatever it is, I can help.'

'No you can't,' said Rob. 'You're only seven!'

'Nearly eight,' Millie said loudly. 'I'm a big girl.'

'Hush!' Rob glanced at the door of the downstairs room where his mother slept. 'You're not coming,' he declared.

'Yes I am.' Millie spoke quietly but very firmly. 'You can't stop me.'

'I'm going to see if I can find out about Dad.' Rob pointed to the clock on the wall. 'And I need to go quickly across the fields to reach the hill at Glebe Farm in time.'

'You carry on. I'll follow as fast as I can.'

'No!' Rob snapped at her.

Nell made a low noise in her throat, looking from Rob's face to his sister's. Rob put his hand on the dog's head. He knew she got upset when he and his sister argued.

'Millie,' he said more kindly, 'I'm four, almost five years older than you. And . . . and it's a boy's thing to do – to go and search for his father.'

Millie looked up at her brother. 'He's my daddy too,' she said.

Rob gazed at his little sister. 'So he is,' he said finally. 'So he is.'

Beside him he felt the dog relax at the change in his tone of voice. He sighed. 'C'mon, then,' he said to Millie. 'We'll have to hurry.'

CHAPTER THREE

Nell slipped ahead of them as they stepped outside their cottage.

Rob took the storm lantern that hung on a nail by the door and lit it with the burning taper he'd stuck in the embers of the kitchen fire. Then he and Millie followed the dog to the nearby shed.

Inside, among a pile of straw, Nell's puppies were nestled together in balls of black and white. Millie picked up the puppy Rob had promised she could have for herself. She hadn't yet thought of what to call him and was trying out various names.

'Rex . . .' she murmured. 'Do you like that name,

little doggie?' She nuzzled the puppy's cheek. 'Do you?'

With a wobbly wriggle the puppy put out a small pink tongue to lick Millie's fingers.

'See!' she said in delight. 'My dog is beginning to know me already. He turned his head at the sound of my voice.'

'I'm not surprised,' Rob said. 'You're in here every day cuddling him. Put him back. We have to get on.'

Millie knelt to replace the puppy in the straw. Then she straightened up and threw her arms around Rob's waist. 'Thank you, Robbie,' she said. 'Thank you for giving him to me. You're the best brother in the whole world.'

Rob unwrapped his sister's arms. 'We'd better move.'

'And you are the best puppy dog,' Millie told the pup, who was now being licked in turn by his mother.

'What do you think of "Lallans" for a name, Rob?' asked Millie as they left the pups and began to walk towards the hill behind their house. 'Do you think that would suit him?'

'Maybe,' Rob said.

'That's where we live, isn't it? Dad said "Lallans" means the Lowlands. When people talk about Scotland, they always think of the Highlands. But the Lowlands are just as important. Here in the Borders we've got the best land for crops and animals. Dad told me that.'

Rob remembered their dad telling them lots of things – like how the fields around their cottage got their names. Dad said that his grandfather had called the fields after places he'd seen, such as Africa and India, when he'd gone to be a soldier in the British Army.

Rob's dad had been in the Reserves. 'Playing with guns,' his mum had said, laughing – never thinking that he'd be called upon to fight in a real war. Although Dad hadn't been called up, exactly. He'd wanted to go. Right from the start, when war was declared, he was keen to be part of it.

Rob remembered his parents talking by the fire one night.

'I'd not be away long.' His dad had a wheedling tone to his voice. 'They say it'll be over by Christmas.'

'You've always hankered to travel the world, haven't you?' his mum replied. 'You listened to the adventure stories of your granddad and now you want to see those places for yourself.'

Rob heard the big chair creak. He could picture the scene in his head. His mum, sitting on the low stool by the fire, brushing her hair out before going to bed. His dad, leaning forward to take the hairbrush and do it for her.

His mum was smiling, but concerned. 'You want to try out army life, but war isn't a game, William.'

'I know, love, I know. But I'd be in the reserves, guarding the supply units. We'd be well in the rear as the main army advances.'

His mum sighed. 'Go, if you must. It might get it out of your system. I think Rob and I can cope with the farm work here for a bit.'

'Don't worry about that. Old Tam will manage the hill sheep on his own. He's been shepherding nigh on sixty years. And I'll rent out our crop fields to Farmer Gordon. I won't be gone long. It'll be over in weeks,' his dad had assured her. 'A couple of months at most.'

But it wasn't over in a couple of months. And his dad's unit didn't stay safe in the rear. The British Army never advanced much. The opposite happened. They were forced to fall back. So the soldiers dug trenches to try and stop the enemy coming forward. The trenches stretched in a line across France and Belgium, and that area became the battlefields the newspapers named the Western Front. Christmas passed, and then another, with more and more months of hard, bitter fighting. Rob's dad wrote to his mum constantly, with extra notes specially for Rob and Millie.

Until, one day, the letters stopped.

Missing him was a horrible big achy Dad-shaped space in life, Rob thought. He reached out his hand and, sensing his mood, Nell came to him at once. The dog seemed to know that silence was required and, although keen to have a run across the fields, she kept close by him.

'Stay by me,' Rob said. 'Good dog.'

They went round the edge of the first field, the one called Africa. Before the war started, when passing this way,

Rob and Millie would pretend they were travelling through the real Africa. They'd wipe sweat from their brows and play make-believe that there were dangerous lions and elephants among the long grass. But now, with the telegram arriving, it was as if it wasn't right to have fun any more. Rob increased his pace.

Millie chatted as she trotted beside him. As usual, any conversation with her was a constant stream of questions.

'Will my dog be able to do everything Nell does?' she asked her brother as they opened the gate to the pasture land. 'Like herd sheep, and fetch things for me?'

'You'll have to train him, but he should understand what you want. His sire was pure bred and Nell is the smartest dog in the world.'

'Why are we going to the hill at Glebe Farm?' Millie went on. 'Is it because the railway line is there? Are we getting on a train?'

He should have realized that Millie would work out what he was doing. Even though she was young, she was

14

really brainy. Always got top marks in tests at school – better than Rob ever did.

'I'm . . . we are not getting on a train,' he answered her. 'But yes, we are going to watch for a train – a certain type of train. It's called a hospital train. I heard that they've converted train carriages into units for wounded soldiers. The ships bring them across the Channel from France and then they're put onto trains to take them straight to hospitals in the big cities of Britain.'

'But Rob, are you sure we'll see a hospital train on *our* railway line?'

'The line going up the hill past Glebe Farm carries on into Edinburgh, and one of the big hospitals there has been made into an army hospital. I was in the post office and I heard Mrs Shelby reading it out from the newspaper. She said they'd have special trains bringing our wounded home so that they could get proper medical care and be near their loved ones. It's been well organized, she said. "Good to know our boys are being looked after." That's what she said.'

'Yes, but how do you know the train is coming through this morning?'

'Kenneth told me. His dad works on the railway, so he knows. He said they're running the hospital train at this time so as not to be in the way of the normal daytime trains.'

'How did Kenneth know that our daddy would be on this train?'

'He doesn't, and neither do I. But the soldiers on the train will have come from the battlefields, and I think some should be from Dad's regiment.'

'Oh, I see what you mean!' exclaimed Millie. 'If the wounded soldiers are being sent to their loved ones, then the ones from Dad's regiment will come to Edinburgh. You are so clever, Rob, to work that out.'

Rob grinned at her. Usually he was better at doing things with his hands than with his head, but he was pleased with himself for coming up with this idea.

'How will we get to talk to them?' Millie was out of breath and Rob slowed to answer her.

'I reckon they'll reduce speed on the hill like every train

does. Then we'll run alongside and call out to the men. We can shout out our father's battalion and see if anyone knows him.'

'Oh, someone will know him,' Millie said confidently. 'Daddy is such a nice man, and very friendly, always singing songs. I'll bet he's made lots of friends.'

Rob looked at his sister. He didn't want to crush her hopes, but he knew that it was a bit far-fetched to think that anyone on the train would have actually met their father personally. But it was reasonable to hope that there would be someone from his regiment. Lots of men from round these parts – from Glendale and the neighbouring towns and villages – had enlisted in the same regiment, the Border Guards. Rob reckoned that when they were sorting them out as they carried them from the ships, they'd send the men to their regiment's recruiting area. That would mean the Border Guards would be on the train going to the hospital in Edinburgh.

The sheep scattered as they ran across the grazing lands, their white shapes fuzzy in the breaking dawn. Light was shining from the kitchen of Glebe Farm. Mr Gordon would be getting ready to milk his cows as his wife put the bread dough in the oven. Now they were at the hill and they could see the wide spread of the crop fields, the woods and meadows of the rolling Lowlands.

Then, in the distance, a blow of red sparks rose high into the air with billows of smoke and steam. A chugging, rattling noise, getting louder and louder.

Racing towards them was a train. A very long train, the engine going full blast and pulling behind it a great many carriages.

'Oh no!' Rob cried. 'We're too late! We're going to miss the train!'

CHAPTER FOUR

Despair swept over Rob.

This had been a chance in a million. There probably wouldn't be another train for months after this, and when the next one was due, he might not be able to find out the day and time it was coming.

'Don't get upset,' Millie said.

'I'm not!' Rob scrubbed his face hard with his hand. He kicked a clod of earth, and turned and stamped off the way they had come.

'Rob!' Millie ran after him. 'Come back!'

'No!' Rob yelled. It was *her* stupid fault that they'd missed the train. She'd made him late. Playing daft games with puppies when there was something really important to do, and then chattering on, distracting him, and making him walk slowly. He bit his lip to keep in the angry words he wanted to shout at his sister.

'Please!' Millie caught up with him, but Rob only walked faster. 'Look, Rob!' she cried. 'The train is stopping!'

At that, he swivelled round and saw that it had indeed stopped a few hundred yards short of the hill.

'There are faces at the windows. And . . . Oh! Some people are getting out!'

Rob didn't hear the rest of what Millie was saying. He was already running down the hill towards the railway track. By the time he reached the train, a soldier was standing beside the engine talking to the driver.

'Engine's overheating,' Rob heard the driver say as he approached. 'We need to take on water or we'll never make that hill and the last run in to Edinburgh. I was told this was the place to make a halt.' He spotted Rob. 'There's a local lad – he might know where there's a water tank hereabouts.'

'I don't,' Rob said quickly, and then spoke directly to the

soldier. 'I'm looking for my dad. He's gone missing in the war. Soldiers from the Border Guards should be on this train. Can you tell me which carriage they'd be in?'

'What are you talking about, son?'

'My dad enlisted in the local regiment, the Border Guards,' Rob explained. 'It was in the newspapers that hospital trains are bringing wounded soldiers home, so the army would take anyone in the Border Guards here to Edinburgh.'

The soldier gave Rob a strange look. 'Oh, that's a real take-on, so it is.'

'What do you mean?' he asked.

'That you think that might happen. We enlisted as pals together, but many a friend I've left behind at the Front—' The soldier's voice cracked. 'Did you think we'd all be singing "Goodbye, Dolly Gray" as they carried us off the battlefield?'

'My name's Millie and my daddy's a very good singer.' Millie had arrived, and was smiling up at the soldier. 'He'd be able to sing that song.'

The man looked at her. 'Listen, pet . . .' he began. He passed his hands across his face. 'Darlin' little girl,' he started again, 'your daddy . . .' He made a choking noise in his throat.

Rob looked at the man in shock. He was crying. He had never seen a man cry before. Except one of their neighbours, Farmer MacAdam, who'd burst into tears when his bull won first prize at the cattle show, but that didn't really count. This man was a soldier. Soldiers weren't supposed to cry. There were tears on his cheeks but he didn't seem to be aware of it.

'Pull yourself together, man,' the engine driver chided the soldier. 'Why don't you walk to that farm on the hill with my fireman and ask if there's water available? The exercise will do you good.' He jabbed his finger at Rob. 'I've got my eye on you, my lad. Don't you go trying to get on my train.'

Rob took Millie's hand and pulled her away. Drat! He'd been too hasty. He should have thought out what he was going to do. He noticed that a couple more soldiers had got off the train in the company of a nurse. Rob recognized her uniform from his collection of war magazines.

'Do you see those people?' he whispered to Millie.

She nodded.

'The lady is wearing a nurse's outfit with the red cape of the Queen Alexandra nurses, so she must be working on the train. We'll go and talk to them. While I keep them chatting, you sneak behind and climb into one of the carriages. Once you're inside, ask where the soldiers from the Border Guards regiment are on the train. When you find out, go straight to that carriage and . . . and . . .'

'I'll take the tea towel from my basket and wave it out the window so you'll know where I am,' Millie finished the sentence for him.

'Yes, that's a good idea,' Rob agreed. 'Do you think you can do that?'

'Of course,' Millie said, and then added, 'I told you I'd be helpful.'

She skipped to the side of the track to gather wild flowers and put them in her basket. Rob saw that she was moving beyond the group. He had to concede that his little sister *was* being helpful.

As Millie sidled off, he saw that the two men wore the staff-and-serpent collar badge of medical orderlies. He asked them the same question he'd asked the first soldier about his father.

'There are trains going to the military hospitals in lots of different parts of Britain,' one of the men replied. 'Why did ye think yer dad might be on this particular train?'

"Cos it's bound for Edinburgh,' Rob told him, 'and they'd put the men that lived here on it so they'd be near their families.'

The orderly laughed out loud. But it wasn't a nice laugh. It was harsh and ugly. 'Is that what ye thought? Listen to me, boy. The wounded are lucky to get on any train. They're lucky if they get picked up off the battlefields and not left for the rats to eat them alive. They're lucky if they survive the dressing station. Can you imagine the paperwork? No one's checking their home address when they're slinging them on the ships.'

'I thought . . .'

'What did ye think?' the orderly went on. 'That it were a Sunday School trip? Did yer da think he were off on a picnic? Eh? Did he?'

'Leave him be, Chesney,' the other orderly cut in. 'He's but a boy.'

'I know that, Bert, but we've both seen ones as young as he is out there getting slaughtered.' Chesney twisted away abruptly.

Rob turned to the nurse. 'Please, miss. Can I ask you if anyone from the Border Guards is on the train?'

'Son, things get really mixed up' – the nurse's voice was friendly – 'so there are men from lots of regiments scattered through the train. But despite the paperwork' – she gave the man called Chesney a firm look – 'they do make some attempt to place the soldiers near their homes. We'll sort it out when we reach Edinburgh.'

'But aren't the men from the same regiment together when they're fighting?' Rob thought of the illustrations in his school books where he'd seen the vivid red line of the

British Army uniforms as the soldiers went forward side by side. 'And they'd stick together when in battle. I mean, they'd look out for each other if they got wounded, wouldn't they? The rest wouldn't go and leave them?'

Nobody said anything. Eventually the nurse spoke. 'It can get very busy when the big guns go off.'

'Yes, but afterwards . . .' Rob persisted. 'When the battle stops, or at night, or during a ceasefire, then whoever was bringing the wounded in—'

'The stretcher-bearers . . .' The nurse supplied the word for him.

'The stretcher-bearers,' said Rob. 'The stretcher-bearers who collect the fallen would . . .' His voice tailed off. What *did* happen to the wounded men? He supposed they'd end up in a hospital somewhere, being looked after by nurses and doctors, but he hadn't thought of how they got there.

The nurse was listening to him with a sympathetic expression on her face. 'The first thing the medics do is a wound assessment. In the Casualty Clearing Stations they try to patch up as many as they can as fast as they can and get them back into active service. The rest . . .' She paused. 'Erm, it depends on how badly hurt they are.'

Rob saw her eyes cloud over. He guessed she must have been there, nursing soldiers on the Western Front. 'What is it like – at the Front?' he asked her.

The nurse blinked. 'Oh, look!' she said brightly. 'They seem to be bringing water from that farm on the hill. We should be on our way soon.'

Farmer Gordon was unwinding a hose pipe down the hill and the soldier and the fireman were carrying buckets. Behind the nurse, Rob saw Millie climb up onto the train. He had to keep these three talking to give his sister time to go through the carriages.

'What happens to them then?' Rob asked the nurse.

'When?'

'To the rest of the wounded? The ones they can't patch up. What happens to them?'

'Oh, well, they transport the more seriously wounded men back to base.' She glanced round at her companions, as if for help.

'Why do you want to know about the wounded?' said the orderly called Bert.

'Our dad joined the Border Guards,' Rob answered, 'and he sent letters every day, but then they stopped.'

'Do you know where he was stationed?' Chesney asked.

'The last letter we got, he was near a river called the Somme.'

The men exchanged a look.

'The Somme,' the nurse repeated.

Rob nodded.

'When did he last write to you?'

'Two months ago. Near the end of June. And then—' Rob stopped.

'And then?' the nurse prompted him.

'My mum got . . .' He wanted to tell them about the telegram but couldn't get the words out.

'Did your mother receive a telegram from the War Office?' the nurse asked gently.

'Yes, b-b–but it didn't say Dad was dead,' Rob stuttered. 'It just said he was missing in action.'

'Oh, one of those telegrams,' Chesney said sourly.

'Hush!' The nurse flapped her hand at him. 'The Border Guards are a brave regiment and I'm sure they look after their own. But you know, I don't think there are any Scottish battalions on this train at all.'

'No Border Guards?' Rob asked in surprise. 'In a train bound for the north?'

'I'm afraid that's how it is. Thousands of men have to be evacuated and they're loaded on any which way.'

'Hang on,' Bert said. 'Isn't that young lad in the last carriage a Jock?'

The nurse frowned at him.

'Oh, right enough,' Bert said quickly. 'Never mind him. Definitely not your dad. Far too young. Not much older than you, actually.'

'But if he's a Scot, then he might be from the Border Guards!' Hope flared in Rob. 'Or he might know someone who is.'

'No.' The nurse shook her head. 'He won't be able to help you.'

'May I speak to him please?' Rob begged her.

'Absolutely not,' she said. 'He's too ill to speak to any-one.'

'But—' Rob began to protest, when suddenly from inside the train a soldier appeared.

'Get in here quick,' he shouted at the nurse. 'There's a little girl being held hostage by one of the crazies at the back of the train. He's got a gun and he's threatening to shoot her!'

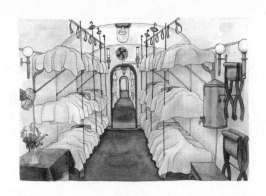

CHAPTER FIVE

'Millie!' Rob cried out.

He rushed towards the train steps, but Chesney grasped his wrists. 'We'll deal with this.'

'She's my little sister!' Rob shouted. 'I need to go to her!'

They paid him no heed. As he struggled to free himself, Bert and the nurse hurried up the steps.

'Wait here. And that's an order.' Chesney pushed him to the ground and went into the train, slamming the door shut.

Rob sat there for a moment, shaking with fear and frustration. Then he recalled that Millie had entered the train further down. He jumped up and raced along the line, away from the engine, to the steps he thought his sister had climbed. There was no way he was leaving Millie alone. It was his duty to look after her. Nell was by his side and took a flying leap after him as he hauled himself up and opened the door of the carriage.

He stopped, brought up short by what he saw. The carriage was packed with wounded men. It seemed to him that they'd been crammed inside the compartments the way he rammed his wooden toy soldiers into their box. Seats and aisles were stacked with dozens and dozens of men, sitting, standing, slumped on the floor, propped up against seats, or leaning against the luggage racks. They were unshaven and dirty, wearing clothes spattered with mud, and wrapped in blood-stained bandages.

Rob knew he had to get through them fast. Chesney and Bert and the nurse would soon catch up with him, coming from the front of the train.

'Excuse me,' he said. Nothing happened. 'Excuse me.' Rob raised his voice. 'I need to go through to the next carriage.'

Nobody moved. It was as if they couldn't see or hear

him. Most of the men had their eyes closed, even the ones who were standing up. Those who were awake stared vacantly out of the window.

Anxiety flooded through Rob. If he didn't get going, Chesney would arrive and fling him off the train.

It was Nell who solved the problem. She barked. A short bark, friendly but firm. The kind of bark she gave to let the sheep know she was there and must do as she wanted, because she wasn't going to put up with any of their nonsense.

The eyes of the nearest man flickered open. 'Dog . . .' he murmured. 'Dog.' He shifted to let Nell past. 'There you go, boy.'

'Thank you,' Rob said, quashing the urge to inform him that Nell was a girl.

Another soldier leaned over and patted Nell. 'Make way, there,' he said. 'Make way for the dog.'

With Nell leading, Rob wormed his way among the soldiers and into the next carriage. There were fewer soldiers here, which made his progress easier, but the men were in a worse state. They were amputees lying on makeshift cots. Rob could see the stump of an arm or a leg, sometimes both, as he manoeuvred along the passage-way. Many of their wounds were coated in congealed blood, with a rust-brown liquid seeping from the dress-ings. Rob was used to farmyard smells, but all around him was an unfamiliar odour of decay and rotting flesh. The stench, combined with stale sweat and urine, almost over-powered him.

A medical orderly, bending to give a soldier a drink of water, looked up as Rob drew level with them. 'You shouldn't be here!'

The man he was tending moaned. 'Morphine. Morphine, please.' His whole chest was swathed in bandages.

'Ain't got none left, soldier.' The orderly patted the man's hand. 'We'll be in Edinburgh soon, then you'll get a pill. I'll see to it myself.'

More men were calling out in pain. The orderly tried to catch Rob by the arm but he evaded him.

'Come back, you!'

Rob stumbled on. All the soldiers in the next carriage sat or knelt on the floor, and every single one had his eyes bandaged. The skin on their faces and hands was blistered orange, their uniforms blotched with greenish stains. Rob tried to shut out the wheezing gurgle of their breathing.

He was living one of his nightmares.

Gripping Nell by her collar, he tried to move as silently as possible so as not to disturb them. But one man shifted position and Nell's coat made contact with the side of his face.

This soldier groped out blindly with his hand, saying in surprise, 'I do believe there's a dog hereabouts.'

'Shut up, Ralph,' one of his companions said. 'If you're going to imagine you can see something, could you make it a pretty girl instead of a dog?'

'No, truly,' Ralph insisted. 'There was the touch of long silky hair against my cheek.'

'Was she blonde?' another man's voice rasped. 'I'd like her to have long blonde ringlets.'

'Oh, dream me up a redhead any day of the week,' said someone else. 'They're much more fun.'

A few of the men tried to laugh, breath catching in their throats as they did so. With relief Rob slipped quietly out of the carriage. His own breath was crackling in his lungs and Nell was panting hard. He gulped in fresh air. Surely he must be near the end of the train now?

The next carriage was horribly silent. The soldiers lay flat out on their backs, so still, barely breathing. This must be the carriage of the most seriously wounded. Rob faltered, but knew he had to continue. He had to find Millie. But what was in the final carriage? What was worse than all he had already seen?

There was no attendant here, so Rob ran straight through and opened the door to face the very last carriage. In front of him was a soldier, his rifle at the ready.

'Stop!' He held up his hand.

Rob hesitated for a second, then dived to the side and dragged open the door. He'd made it right to the end of the train! He was in the guard's van, normally used for boxes and heavy luggage. And there was his sister, standing rigid with terror, clutching her basket of sandwiches.

There were two soldiers inside. One of them was sitting on the floor with his eyes shut, mumbling to himself. He was handcuffed to a metal pole.

The other soldier was free.

He was holding a gun up against Millie's head.

CHAPTER SIX

'Millie!' Rob gasped.

'Robbie,' Millie whispered. 'I knew you'd come to save me.'

Rob stared at her, and then at the young lad with the pistol. The boy's face was dirty grey with a mottled flush high on each cheek. His eyes were red-rimmed and they flashed about, never still.

Rob had cared for farm animals all his life. Normally they were very biddable, but if the sheep were sick or lambing, or a cow was with calf, they became unpredictable, and therefore dangerous – sometimes extremely dangerous. His dad had told him it was because they were frightened and in pain, and the best way to handle them was to try to understand what they were suffering. One bleak night on the hills they had birthed a lamb from a sick ewe. Hunkered down, his father stroked the writhing creature, teaching Rob how to gentle her into allowing him to help: 'Think how you would like to be treated if you were scared and didn't know what was happening to you.'

The lad in front of him was shaking, his whole body trembling so much he could hardly hold the gun steady. Rob felt fear rising in his throat as he realized that the gun might go off and his sister would be killed. And there was nothing he could do.

Apart from what his father might have done.

Rob stepped back, creating a space between himself and the lad. 'It's all right,' he said softly. He held his hands out, palms up. 'It's all right,' he repeated.

He relaxed his body and saw the lad relax slightly too.

'I'm not going to hurt you,' Rob said in the same soft voice. 'I'm not going to do anything at all.'

Behind him the carriage door crashed open. A voice roaring a command. Chesney's voice.

'You! Farm boy. Out of here. At once!'

Without turning round, Rob shook his head. 'I'm not leaving my sister.'

'I told you,' Chesney said through gritted teeth, 'not to get on the train. Now I'm telling you to move aside. Do it!'

'He stays.' The lad with the pistol addressed Chesney. 'But you! You get out or I'll blow your head off! I mean it!' He pointed the gun at the orderly. 'Get out or I'll fire this gun at you!'

There was a silence; then Chesney leaned forward and hissed in Rob's ear, 'If you don't leave I'll have your soldier father put on a charge and locked up for years.'

'You can't put Daddy on a charge and lock him up.' To Rob's astonishment, it was Millie who spoke up. 'He's missing in the war and that's why we're here. To find out if he's on this train.'

'You shouldn't *be* on this train,' Chesney snapped at her. 'Medical orderly! Stand down!'

An army officer and the nurse had appeared at the carriage door.

'Sir,' Chesney protested. 'This boy disobeyed instructions.'

'Stand down,' the officer repeated. 'That's an order.'

Chesney glared at Rob. When he'd gone, the officer leaned against the door, looked around, and then said in mild tones, 'My name is Captain Morrison. I'd be obliged if someone would bring me up to date on this situation.'

There was a silence.

'Anyone at all? Please.'

The soldier tied to the metal rail stopped mumbling and spoke up without opening his eyes. 'Soldier Jack the Lad here is really good at nicking things. Handcuff keys, guns, and such like. He's been planning his escape ever since we got on at Folkestone. When the train stopped, he was ready to leg it when this little girl turns up asking questions about where the regiments are posted. So he decides she's a German spy and—'

'A German spy.' The lad with the gun tightened his grip on the pistol.

'I'm not a German spy!' Millie squeaked.

Nell's tail was down. Until now she'd had the good sense not to make a noise. But reacting to the alarm in Millie's voice, she crouched, growling.

'Quiet, Nell,' said Rob.

The lad with the gun gave a start and looked at the dog. 'Nell?' he said. The gun wavered in his hand. 'Nell?'

Then the most surprising thing happened. Nell stood up and wagged her tail.

'Nell,' the boy said again, more confidently.

And to Rob's amazement, Nell trotted forward to stand quite happily beside the young soldier.

CHAPTER SEVEN

'I could look after that gun for you, son.'

Captain Morrison was first to recover. He held out his hand. The young lad unclenched his grip on the pistol and the officer took it carefully from him.

Rob looked at the floor. He didn't want to watch what happened next. He knew enough about the army to understand that a soldier who threatened an officer with a gun would be arrested and shot at dawn.

But the captain slipped the gun inside his tunic and said to the nurse, 'Give our young soldier some of those knock-out drops you reserve for emergencies. When he's being assessed in Edinburgh, I'll see if we can get him admitted to a psychiatric unit somewhere. Maybe some smart doctor can straighten out his brain. And – oh,' he added, 'I suggest you put a note in his record that he has a special skill for . . . how shall we put it? . . . appropriating unattended objects.' He touched his cap to the nurse and left.

The lad was stroking Nell's coat as though it were the most natural thing in the world.

The nurse and Bert came into the carriage. The nurse said, 'Bert will look after you while I go and make you the best cup of tea you ever had.'

Bert knelt beside the lad. 'You seem to know this dog,' he said.

'It's Nell,' he replied. He kept patting the dog. 'Rob's dog. She's a clever dog. The best sheepdog in the Borders.'

'The dog certainly likes you, Jack,' Bert said.

Rob knelt down too. He looked the lad full in the face. In the stressed and worn features there was something he recognized. 'Jack? Is that your name?' he asked. 'Do I know you? Are you from round these parts?'

The boy didn't reply.

'It's *Jack*!' Millie exclaimed. 'He's the lad from the Otterby farm. We used to meet him on the hills at lambing time and at the sheepdog trials.'

'Jack the Lad,' the handcuffed soldier chimed in. 'Told you so. Should we put on a show to entertain the troops? We've got him and the dog. All we need now is a cow and a beanstalk and we're sorted.'

'You're all right there, Private Ames,' Bert quietened him.

'You reckon so?' The private held up his handcuffed wrist. 'I didn't think this would happen when I joined up.'

'We had to do that for your own protection. When we get to the hospital you'll get proper care.'

'Have they got magic beans there?' Private Ames grimaced. 'That's what we need. Magic beans. A cow, a beanstalk, and some magic beans.' He lapsed into mumbling to himself again. And all the while, Rob noted, he never once opened his eyes.

The nurse returned with two mugs of tea. She gave one to the handcuffed soldier and handed the other one to Jack. He looked at it suspiciously.

'I ain't drinking that,' he said. 'They put stuff in your tea, you know' – he partially covered his mouth with his hand as he spoke to Rob – 'to make you fight. Don't trust them. Don't trust any of them. Tell you lies. Say the wire's been cut. Land mines been cleared. *Advance! Enemy trenches destroyed! Advance! Advance! In line formation. Walk slowly. Shoulder to shoulder. Enemy trenches empty.* But they were waiting with machine guns to mow us down. Lies! Lies!'

Bert and the nurse glanced at each other. It was obvious that Jack was becoming agitated again.

'Would you like a plum-jam sandwich?' Millie took the teacloth off her basket and held it out.

Jack shook his head.

'I made them especially for my daddy in case he was on the train. Plum is his favourite jam and they're very tasty.'

'I'd like one,' the handcuffed soldier said. 'I can smell home-made jam and fresh bread.'

'My mummy made the jam and the bread, but I helped a lot,' Millie told him. She went over and guided his hands to the basket so he could take a sandwich.

'Oh, my,' said the private. 'That's the best food I've had for twelve months and a day.' He smacked his lips loudly with his eyes shut tight.

On sudden inspiration, Rob said, 'Don't forget to give Nell some.' He took a piece of bread and gave it to his dog.

As soon as he saw Nell eating the sandwich, Jack peered into the basket and selected one for himself. Then he lifted his mug and began to drink the tea. Bert and the nurse smiled in relief. The effect was almost immediate. Jack's eyelids drooped, and he slid sideways. The nurse rescued the mug from his limp fingers before it fell onto the floor. Bert went behind Jack and, placing his hands under his shoulders, pulled him along to the furthest part of the carriage. There he handcuffed his wrists to a metal pole.

CHAPTER EIGHT

'Do you have to handcuff Jack like that?' Millie asked in a small voice as the nurse escorted her and Rob back onto the railway track.

'I'm afraid so, pet. Honestly. He's safer that way.'

'And what about the other man? Why is he tied up?'

'Because if we don't, he harms himself. You may have noticed that the skin around his eyes is deeply scratched. If his hands are free, he tears at his eyelids with his nails.'

'What's wrong with his eyes?' Rob asked. 'Why aren't they bandaged up like some of the soldiers on the train?'

'The other soldiers were caught in a gas attack,' said the nurse. 'It would have come over before they had time to get their gas masks on. Their sight has been damaged.' She showed them her blistered hands. 'The Germans are using different types of gas – it burns everything it touches. Medical staff have to be careful when dressing their wounds.'

'That's not fair,' said Millie. 'Gassing people is a nasty thing to do. The Germans must be cruel people.'

'Our side are using it too,' the nurse said in a quiet voice.

'Oh!' Millie became silent.

Rob reached out and took her hand. 'But that soldier hasn't been gassed, has he?' he asked the nurse.

'I don't think there is anything wrong with Private Ames's actual eyesight,' she replied. 'His condition is that he's unable to open his eyelids.'

Millie opened and closed her eyes several times. 'How can someone not open their eyes?'

'The doctors suspect he's in such deep shock that his eyelids are stuck shut.'

In all his reading of war books and listening to his dad's stories Rob had never heard of anything like this.

'What would cause someone's eyelids to stay stuck shut?'

'Maybe it was what he saw.' The nurse looked at Rob and then at Millie. 'If both of you walked through the train, then you've an idea of how bad the battlefields can be. But look,' she said, 'the engine driver is signalling to us. I expect he wants to restart the train so we can get on our way.'

'There's Farmer Gordon,' said Millie. She waved her hand. 'I'll go and say hello.'

As she ran ahead, Rob turned to the nurse and said, 'What did that soldier see that would make him never want to open his eyes again?'

The nurse shook her head.

'Please,' said Rob. 'I'd like to know. As soon as I'm old enough I'll be called up and I need to be prepared.'

She looked at him for a moment. 'In that case I'll tell you, in the hope that it makes you not rush to enlist. If your soldier father has gone missing, then your mother needs you more than ever. You'll have to be a father to your sister until such time as you find out what has happened to your own.' She pointed to where Millie was standing with the farmer and the engine driver and the captain who had taken the gun from Jack Otterby.

'Please tell mc,' said Rob.

'There are boys almost as young as you out there,' said the nurse. 'Ones who lied about their age because they thought that fighting a war would be exciting – a glorious game – and they'd go away with their friends and come home covered in glory. But it is truly awful. There are lice and flies in the trenches, and rats: bloated, filthy creatures. There are no proper lavatories and the food is often bad. The shells churn up the ground and the poor horses flounder in the mud and drown – sometimes soldiers go under too. The bombardment never stops, and the noise of the explosions going on and on, day and night, drives some soldiers crazy. They get confused; everything gets mixed up inside their head. They never know when they might be attacked or gas might drift across. There's constant sniper fire picking off those who forget to keep their head down – we lose quite a number of our new recruits that way. Like most of the men, our soldier, Private Ames, was under an enormous amount of stress. Then there was some action where he witnessed complete carnage and lost every one of his friends. He told me that he closed his eyes because he couldn't bear to watch his comrades being killed, and when he tried to open them again, he couldn't do it. He was in the midst of the worst advance movement of the war so far, a terrible battle near the Somme.'

The Somme!

Rob gasped.

The nurse put her hand to her mouth. 'I'm so sorry! I forgot. That's where your father was stationed.'

They both glanced towards Millie, glad that she was too far away to hear their conversation. The nurse placed her finger over her lips.

'I won't say anything,' said Rob. He realized that he had to keep that information to himself. He mustn't tell Millie . . . or his mother. 'Can't the doctors do anything for Private Ames?'

'Sometimes the soldiers become unwell in their minds. It's not only their bodies that are damaged in war. Bert and

I have spent time talking to both soldiers in the last carriage, and that seems to help, but they need special doctors. I believe they've got a psychiatric unit near Edinburgh where the therapy concentrates on soldiers' minds.'

Rob knew that people got sick in their heads. His grand-dad had lived with them until he died. In his old age he did odd things, getting up in the middle of the night thinking it was daytime. Then there was the postmistress's daughter, Annie, who helped in the school, giving out pencils and tidy-ing up. She was twenty-two, but inside her head she was younger than Millie. But it wasn't the same for Private Ames and Jack. They'd been fine before they'd gone into battle.

'Kindness is important; empathy is what they need – but there's no time for that on the battlefield. And army officers can't afford to appear weak, else there would be no soldiers willing to fight.'

Rob looked to where the captain was standing chatting to the engine driver. 'Captain Morrison is kind,' he said. 'He took the gun from Jack and didn't say anything. He could have put him on a charge.'

'Captain Morrison has a son the same age as Jack fighting on the Front Line. He is more sympathetic to the men's fears than a lot of other officers.'

Captain Morrison noticed them approaching. He broke off his conversation to come and speak to them. 'I'd like a word with you, young man. Your sister was in extreme danger earlier.'

'I'm sorry we caused so much trouble,' Rob said. 'Millie's not to blame for what happened. She was only doing what I asked her to do. I told her to get on the train when no one was looking and try to find out anything she could about the Border Guards. It was my fault that Jack mistook her for a German spy and—'

'All right. All right.' Captain Morrison held up his hand. 'Apology accepted. I'm given to understand that you are trying to trace your father who is missing in the war?'

'Yes, sir, we are.'

'I'm guessing your mother does not know that you and your sister left home to go off on an adventure at half past five in the morning?'

Rob's heart flipped in alarm. 'No, sir, she does not.'

'I'm further guessing that you'd prefer that she was not informed.'

Rob looked pleadingly at the nurse and then at the captain. 'Mother has been unwell since the telegram arrived, sir. I don't want her to have any more worry.'

'I see.' The captain studied Rob. 'I'll make a pact with you. I will say nothing to anyone regarding the incident on the train, and I will further instruct all personnel involved to remain silent, on condition that you and your sister do likewise.'

Rob nodded. 'Yes, sir,' he said in relief.

'I also do not want you to speak of what you saw as you went through the carriages. The condition of wounded soldiers is classified information.'

'I understand, sir.'

'I hope you do. Even though Private Otterby is having delusions and exhibiting signs of paranoia, he is in fact correct when he says there are German spies around. Any information concerning wounded men and battle conditions would be of great use to the enemy. You must remain silent on this subject.'

'I will say nothing about the soldiers on the train,' Rob promised, 'and neither will Millie. You can rely on us.'

'That will not be an easy thing for either of you,' said the captain.

'If I may make a suggestion, Captain Morrison?' asked the nurse.

'Indeed, yes, Nurse Evans.'

'I am from a rural area where everyone knows the business of everyone else. With us stopping to take on water, it won't be any secret that a hospital train passed this way. It might be best if the children are allowed to say that they saw the train and waved to the men, but leave out the part where they actually got on.'

'Excellent idea,' the captain agreed. 'Especially as it looks as if this will be a regular stop for future trains. The engine driver says he'll file a report advising that a water tank with a mechanical hose system be constructed here.' He took a notebook out of his pocket and gave it to Rob. 'Write your father's details and your home address and I'll make such enquiries as I can for you.'

'Thank you, sir,' said Rob, jotting them down before handing back the notebook.

Captain Morrison looked at him. 'I suppose I'll see you again at some point, but you must give me your word that neither you nor your sister will ever attempt to board a hospital train again.'

'Yes,' said Rob. 'I do.' He gave the captain his best salute, exactly as his father had shown him.

Captain Morrison returned the salute and went up the steps and onto the train.

'So every hospital train on its way to Edinburgh will stop here!' Rob said to Nurse Evans.

'It would seem so. But you mind what you promised the captain,' she warned him. 'You'll never get on the train again.'

'Yes,' said Rob, 'but *you'll* be on the train, won't you?'

'I expect so, but in time there may be more going up the line and I can't be on each one. You do appreciate after what you've learned today . . . it's not very likely that there will be anyone on the trains who'd have information about your father?'

Rob felt tears building behind his eyes. 'It's completely hopeless, isn't it?'

'No,' the nurse replied, 'I wouldn't say that. I've seen men recover from the most grievous wounds. Nursed a soldier through the night, never expecting him to see another dawn, and then he sits up in bed and eats a full breakfast. So I never say anything is hopeless.'

'What should I hope for, then?'

'That I cannot tell you. But know this: today you met a nurse called Ethel Evans, and for as long as I'm detailed duty on this hospital train run, I will check through the carriages on the way north. If there is any news of your father, I'll give a signal from one of the carriage windows. That's the best I can do.'

The train whistle sounded.

'Looks like we're going.' To Rob's embarrassment, before getting on the train Nurse Ethel Evans gave him a quick hug. 'Take care of your mother,' she told him. 'And your sister.'

Rob went to join Millie, who was now genuinely gathering wild flowers.

'I'll bring these to Mummy,' she said. 'She likes flowers. And if she's up when we get home, then we can say that's why we went out this morning.'

'Good idea,' said Rob, marvelling again at how smart his little sister was.

Farmer Gordon was still speaking to the engine driver and the fireman, so Rob pretended to help Millie while listening to their conversation.

'I recall my own father telling me that the royal train stopped here to take on water,' Farmer Gordon was saying. 'There's a piping system close by.' He pointed to the edge of the track. 'A couple of your railway workers will be able to fix that up again. It's been neglected because the passenger trains make the gradient with no bother.'

'This engine's been pulling all the way from Folkestone.'

'Aye, and it's a fair length. But I'll warrant you'll not have so much again. If the big engagements are over, our boys will have sent them packing. It'll be mopping-up operations until the end of the year.'

The driver shook his head. 'Ours is not the only train. There's ones going to all the big cities. They'll be others coming this way, maybe with even more carriages. Our lads are suffering heavy losses.'

Mr Gordon raised his eyebrows. 'That's not the word we're getting. Newspapers say we're making advances.'

'The German Army has dug in and their defences are better than ours. Any of the more experienced lads will tell you.' The train driver lowered his voice. 'They say it's treason to talk that way – but unless we know, how can we defend ourselves? The enemy have burrowed deep into the earth and built bunkers made of solid concrete. They hide there until the shelling stops, and our boys go forward thinking there will be no resistance. That's when the Hun comes out with his machine guns at the ready.'

'One big push, that's what we thought. One more big push and it would be over.'

'We've given them more than one big push and they don't budge. A mile into no-man's-land, and then we're driven back. That's how it seems to be going. It'll be a few more years yet,' said the driver, 'unless the Americans come in.'

'We thought it was nearing the end,' said Farmer Gordon. 'You reckon there will be another hospital train soon after this one?'

'With what's going on over there, there will be trains coming through here every other week.'

CHAPTER NINE

Rob picked a switch from a nearby tree to help Farmer Gordon guide his cows to the milking shed. Nell moved to prevent one wandering off round the side of the farmhouse.

'She's a capable dog, your Nell,' said the farmer.

'She is that,' Rob said proudly.

'And her litter must be weaned. Those pups will fetch a good price, so yer mam will have some extra money coming in.'

Rob wasn't happy that Nell's pups would have to be sold. But he was old enough to understand it had to happen. He thought of the smallest pup, the one he'd given

Millie. At least they would have that one to keep.

Millie leaned her head against the side of the first cow as the farmer settled himself on a low stool.

'No word of yer dad?' he asked.

Rob shook his head.

'Aye, well, ye never know.' He squirted the warm milk into the pail. 'Go on into the house,' he said. 'Mrs Gordon has some scones left over from last night. Better you get them than those greedy ducks of mine.'

Millie and Rob went across the yard and peered over the half-door to see Mrs Gordon energetically kneading a lump of dough. She caught sight of them and smiled.

'Mr Gordon said to call by—' Rob stopped, not wanting to mention the scones.

'Come in.' Mrs Gordon beckoned to them. 'Come in.' She observed them shrewdly. 'Oh my, look at that porridge pot of mine. Overflowing as always. I never get the measures right since my lass got married and moved away. Let me put some out for you to sup up.' She scooped dollops of porridge into bowls and poured fresh milk on top.

Millie didn't hesitate. Taking a spoon from the kitchen drawer, she sat herself upon a chair and began to eat.

'What else have I got here?' Mrs Gordon bustled about her kitchen. 'Oh, there's my baking trays from yesterday. I always make too much. Ye'd be doing me a favour by eating these, so ye would. Our ducks are sick of my scones.'

'I can leave you some sandwiches spread with my mummy's plum jam,' Millie offered.

'Fair exchange!' Mrs Gordon clapped her hands. 'Although I think I'm taking advantage of you, Millie Gowrie. Your mother's plum jam is famed on both sides of the Border.' She glanced at them as she spread thick butter on the scones. 'How is your mother doing, then?'

Millie kept her head bent over her bowl.

'Fine,' Rob said. 'She's fine.'

Mrs Gordon smiled cheerfully at them. 'That's the spirit,' she said. 'Oh, look, take the rest of these. Sam and I will never eat them.' She dropped the rest of the scones into Millie's basket. 'That'll do you for your school piece today.'

Rob gobbled the remainder of his porridge. 'We need to

go now, thank you.' If they didn't leave soon, Mrs Gordon would empty her whole larder into Millie's basket.

'Mind and tell your mum I was asking for her. Don't forget.'

'We will,' Millie said. 'And thank you very much.'

They returned over the fields at a slower pace, Rob carrying a small churn full of fresh milk, which was his regular morning errand to Glebe Farm. With the sun over the horizon they could see smoke rising in slow columns from the chimneys of houses and farmsteads. It looked so ordinary and peaceful that it was hard to believe that, not so far away across the English Channel, a war was being fought.

Rob's friend Kenneth brought his dad's copy of the *War Illustrated* magazine into school after his dad had finished reading it. All the boys pored over it to look at the pictures. The cover of the recent edition had a photo of a soldier comforting his horse as shells exploded around them. The reporter had been at the Battle of the Somme. He had said that the British Army was advancing. Rob recalled the actual phrase: *Losses count for nothing. We are advancing.*

But this wasn't what was really happening. The driver of the hospital train and Jack Otterby and Nurse Ethel Evans were saying something completely different. And the soldier, Private Ames, had closed his eyes tight shut because he couldn't bear to see what was happening. Nurse Evans said he'd been on the battlefields of the Somme. The Somme . . . That was the river Rob's father had mentioned in his letters.

His dad had written of his pride in being part of a parade – of seeing a general on his horse, taking the salute as the battalion marched past, singing. He'd told of the camaraderie of the men, sharing food sent from home when rations were low; of the games of cricket and football; of the sense of devotion to a just cause. Their undying resolve to defend the Belgian villagers who, despite having very little, gave the soldiers everything they could. He described seeing the French cuirassiers one morning, jangling along the road, glittering in their steel breastplates and high plumed helmets. They were on their way to defend a town called Verdun.

'*Ils ne passeront pas!*' they had cried as they galloped along, brandishing their sabres. '*Ils ne passeront pas.*'

If Verdun fell, then the Germans would enter Paris, the capital of France, and they'd get behind the Allied lines. The enemy could reach the Channel ports; if that happened, all supplies and troops coming in from Britain would be cut off. The war would be lost.

So the British soldiers cheered the French cavalry with a mighty '*Huzzah!*' as they went past. The Tommies threw their caps in the air and joined in their chorus:

'*Ils ne passeront pas! They shall not pass!*'

With a chill descending in his heart Rob realized that his dad's letters hadn't told the truth – not the whole truth, anyway. There was nothing about the rats and the lice, and the defeats. He didn't say what had happened to the friends he didn't mention any more: Arthur who made the jokes, Davey who played the harmonica, and Dan and Andrew. To begin with his letters were full of their antics and the tricks they played on each other. Latterly he hadn't even mentioned their names.

Perhaps that's why his mother had become so silent and listless. She spent time reading and re-reading the letters from the Front. Perhaps she was able to read what wasn't there as well as what was. A chink of understanding came to Rob of why his mother found it hard to rise in the mornings, of why she'd taken to lying longer and longer in her bed. Sometimes, in the night, he heard the muffled sound of her weeping.

He'd been doing more and more of the work she'd normally do and had asked her to write a letter to his teacher so that he could be excused school for farm work. But she refused. On this she was firm:

'No. Your dad and I want you to have an education. You're to remain in school, Rob. No matter what happens.' The words seemed to catch in her throat. 'No matter what happens, you will have an education.'

He'd have to get a move on. There were things to be done this morning before he and Millie set off for school.

They were halfway down the last hill and Rob was

going over his work list in his mind when Nell lifted her head and gave a sharp warning bark.

Rob surveyed the meadow. There was no sheep lying on its back needing to be turned, no lamb tangled in a thorn bush.

'What is it?' he asked her.

Millie knelt and put her arms around the dog's neck. 'What's wrong, Nell?' She looked around. 'I can't see anything amiss.'

'A dog's hearing is much keener than ours,' said Rob. 'She hears something that we can't.' He looked again at Nell.

The dog's nose was pointing towards their cottage. She barked again, this time much louder.

Without saying another word Rob and Millie started to run.

CHAPTER TEN

'You have no authority to do this!'

Rob heard his mother's voice raised in anger as he and Millie raced round the corner of the house. Nell had already taken up a position at the cottage door in front of his mother, protecting her.

'It's an order from the government.' The county vet was standing in their yard holding up an official-looking document. 'This gives me the authority. The War Office is requisitioning animals, and vets have to identify suitable livestock. It's not something I want to do, but I must carry out these instructions.'

'Most of the horses have already gone from hereabouts,'

his mother replied. 'How do they expect the farmers to bring in the harvest without them?'

'Glebe Farm has still got one good working horse, and anyway, it's not horses they want this time. It's dogs.'

'You can't take our dog!' Rob told him.

'I'm not here for your dog. Nell's too old for what's required, but she's a very intelligent animal. I've seen her perform at the sheepdog trials and I know she had a litter a month or so ago. It's the pups you'll have to hand over.'

'The pups?' Millie looked from the vet to Rob. 'Don't let him take Nell's pups, Rob. Don't let him take my puppy dog away to the war.'

'Look . . .' The vet spoke in a reasonable voice. 'Nell will have more puppies. And the army pays out for any livestock taken. I'll mark these as best quality to make sure you get a good price.'

'The pups are not for sale,' said Rob.

'Mrs Gowrie,' said the vet, 'this is a bit of income for you to keep things going. Maybe buy shoes for the children, with winter not far off...'

Rob stole a glance at his mother. Millie's toes were cramped in her shoes and his boots were worn down at both heels.

His mother shook her head. 'The pups are not for sale,' she said, echoing Rob's words.

The vet tilted his head to one side, a look of pity on his face. Suddenly Rob saw his mother through the eyes of someone else. Her long beautiful hair, which his dad loved to brush, was normally plaited and pinned round her head with curls framing her face – 'like an angel', his dad would say. Now it lay, straggly and unkempt, on her shoulders. Her blouse had a stain on it, her apron strings were untied.

'I apologize for any inconvenience this is causing you,' the vet went on. 'But you... we don't have a choice. Everyone has to make sacrifices for the war effort.' He turned the document over in his hand. 'I've to list the description and number of suitable animals on this form. If I don't do it properly, I could lose my job.'

'We're not telling you where they are,' Millie said defiantly. 'And you can't make us.'

'Then I'll have to find them myself.' He took a step forward.

'Do not step inside my home.' Rob's mother put her arm across the door to bar his way. 'Ours is not a tied cottage, it belongs to this family. It was gifted to my husband's grandfather more than a hundred years ago by the earl of this land for his loyal service as a soldier, and I have the papers to prove it. We own it outright and I forbid you to enter.'

The vet tutted in exasperation. 'This only delays things. The Army Procurement Officer is due in this area to-morrow and I'm supposed to have all the paperwork ready for him. I'll have to let him know that you've refused to co-operate, and the army might be less respectful of your rights.'

'We have no information to give you.' Rob and Millie went to stand on either side of their mother as she held firm in the doorway of their cottage.

It was Nell herself who told the vet what he wanted to know.

Seeing that no one was in any danger, she trotted off to the outhouse to check on her pups. The vet strode after her.

'Five pups.' He'd already counted them and was marking the number on his form by the time Rob and Millie got there. 'You should be proud of the work your pups will do,' he told them. He went into the yard and spoke to their mother. 'Dogs have a crucial role in carrying communications when radio contact isn't possible. Yours are young enough to train as messenger dogs.'

'It takes weeks to train a dog. I thought this war was supposed to be over in weeks,' Rob's mother said bitterly. 'They keep telling us that it won't be long. But they've been saying that for two years.'

The vet looked away. 'My own son is out there. Letters are censored, but he's an officer so his are less so. He says that things are not as reported in the newspapers. Conditions are grim, survival rates for the wounded are low—' He stopped as Rob's mum gasped and her hand fluttered to her throat.

'I'm sorry, Mrs Gowrie. I heard you got a telegram from the War Office. I offer my sympathy. But here's where this situation could help you. It can take a while before the army pay out on a widow's pension. With your man gone, you'll be glad of the money for the pups.'

'Our dad isn't dead!' Rob shouted.

'Son—' the vet began.

'He isn't! He isn't! He isn't!' Millie shrieked. 'Daddy isn't dead. You mustn't say it and you mustn't take Nell's puppies.' She ran over and kicked the vet on the leg.

Within seconds Nell had appeared from the outhouse and was beside them, teeth bared and snarling.

The vet backed off quickly. 'Don't take this attitude when the army comes to collect them,' he advised. 'You'll only give yourself more trouble if you resist.' He climbed onto his horse and gathered the reins into his hands. As he rode off he called over his shoulder, 'The Army Procurement Officer will be along in a couple of days to take the puppies away.'

CHAPTER ELEVEN

After the vet left, Rob's mother looked at the children helplessly and put her hands over her face. When Millie's crying got louder, she went back into her bedroom and shut the door.

In the hope that his mother might get up later and want to eat something, Rob poured milk from the churn into a jug. He made a sandwich and left it, and a clean cup, on the kitchen table.

'Stay!' he told Nell. He pointed at the bedroom door. 'Stay! On guard!'

She went and lay down outside it. Rob knew that Nell would look after his mother while he was at school.

He tapped gently on the bedroom door. 'I've left milk and food out for you.' He waited. There was no reply. Rob opened the paper bag Mrs Gordon had given him, took out one scone and laid it on the table. 'Millie and I were up at Glebe Farm this morning,' he called out. 'Mrs Gordon says to tell you she was asking after you. She sent you a scone. Nell's outside your bedroom door. She wants you to share it with her.' Rob waited, but there was only silence inside the room.

'We're off to school, then. Goodbye!'

Rob could not get Millie to stop crying. Finally he picked her up from where she sat on their doorstep and half carried her into the village to the schoolhouse. The old shepherd, Tam, who was looking after his dad's flock while he was away, was waiting by the railings.

'Young Robert Gowrie.' He touched his cap. 'I'm told there's a "killed in action" casualty list been put up outside the post office this morning. Will you come and look at it for me?'

'I'll be late for school,' Rob said. He hated being late for school. The teacher, Miss Finlay, was very strict about time-keeping. His dad had said it was because her father was a sergeant-major in the army. They were the ones who shouted commands and kept the men in line. Rob's teacher made the boys salute and the girls curtsey to her in the morning as they filed past into the school. 'The apple doesn't fall far from the tree,' his dad had joked.

But the old shepherd was very insistent. 'You can read, can't you?'

'Of course I can!' said Rob.

'My son sends me one of those army postcards every week. I haven't heard from him in a month. Maybe something has happened. Even if it's bad news, I'd like to know.'

Rob crossed the street to where the list was pinned to a weathered notice board. Already some villagers were clustered round.

'I'm getting the boy here to look for my son's name,' the old shepherd explained to them. 'My eyesight is not as good as it was.'

'Nor is mine,' said a voice.

'Can you read out the whole list?' someone asked. 'There's a good lad.'

Rob looked into the post office, hoping for help, but Mrs Shelby, the postmistress, was busy with a queue of customers.

'You go on, Millie,' he said to his sister. 'Your friends Pearl and Daisy are waiting for you. Tell the teacher I'm going to be late.'

Rob started to read the casualty list. He'd only called out six names when, from the back of the group, a young woman screamed. Rob knew her. She'd been married last year and was expecting a baby any day. She began to cry, sobbing loudly.

'Are you sure?' The older woman beside her pushed her way to the front. 'Are you sure? Show me. Show me where it says his name.'

Rob pointed to the line.

'Spell it out,' she said.

Letter by letter, Rob spelled out her son's name.

'Ah.' She placed her hands over her heart. 'It's true, then.'

She put her arm round the shoulder of her pregnant daughter-in-law and helped her away.

Rob called eight more names before the same thing happened. Another woman came forward and asked him to point out her brother's name. And so it went on – brother, son, husband, father identified – and the bereaved relative departing in despair. Then Rob realized that there was nothing wrong with their eyesight. The reason they'd asked him to read the list was because many people in the village could not read.

Keeping his voice as steady as he was able, he got to the end. Of the twenty or so who had been gathered there, only three remained. The old shepherd, Tam, was not one of them.

When Rob finally arrived at the school, his teacher didn't give him a row. She merely nodded her head and indicated for him to sit down. His pal Kenneth whispered that someone had told her that Rob was standing out-side the post office reading out the 'killed in action' list.

Annie, the assistant, had already filled the inkwells

from the big jar of ink beside the sink. Brow furrowed in concentration, she carried the rack from row to row to replace the full inkwell in each desk. As she passed down the aisle Jed, a boy who sat opposite Rob, deliberately nudged her so that the tray wobbled. The ink slopped over, dripping onto the floor.

'Oh! Oh! Look what I've done. I've gone and spilled the ink.' Annie's bottom lip trembled. She looked anxiously towards Miss Finlay.

Rob glared at Jed. Trust him to pick on someone weaker than himself.

'Lay off!' Kenneth hissed at Jed.

Rob grabbed a piece of blotting paper and mopped up the puddle of ink.

Annie gave the boys a big smile.

But Miss Finlay was restless this morning. She had a handkerchief in her hand and was twisting it constantly between her fingers. The class was on alert for anything out of the ordinary in their teacher's manner. It usually signalled a test or tables or a visit from a school inspector. All these were torture for Rob, for he wasn't good at most school work.

Miss Finlay stood up, straightened her shoulders, patted her already perfectly groomed hair, and clapped her hands. 'I think we might do some singing,' she announced.

'*Singing.*' Kenneth mouthed the word at Rob. They never had singing first thing in the morning. It was kept as a treat for after hard work, like sums or writing practice.

'That's correct,' Miss Finlay said briskly. 'I've said that the younger classes may engage in free art work today. While they get on with that, the top classes will sing.' She went over to the piano in the corner and flung open the lid.

Annie picked up a stack of song books from the windowsill and passed them out.

Miss Finlay crashed some chords. 'I'd like you to sing really loudly so that everyone in the village' – she paused – 'indeed, everyone in the whole country, can hear you.'

At lunch time their teacher surprised them again by saying, 'You may have extra playtime. I think it would be good for the village to hear children laughing on a day like this.'

Rob and Kenneth found a quiet space in the school yard to sit and talk.

Kenneth already knew that the hospital train had actually stopped in the valley. 'My dad heard his bosses mention it. They reckoned that the engine wouldn't be able to make it up Glebe Hill without taking on more water. The engine drivers have been told not to stop at public railway stations. It might upset people to see so many wounded soldiers.'

'Mr Gordon said there used to be a water tank there,' Rob said.

Kenneth nodded. 'My dad says there's to be a proper water tank with a mechanical pump built below Glebe Hill so in the future the hospital trains can stop there. They're expecting more coming up from the south soon.'

More trains already! Rob's heart rate quickened. Although he felt sorry for the men who were wounded, more trains meant more chances of finding out about his dad. Rob longed to let his friend know what he'd seen on the train, but he knew he mustn't. Instead, he told him about Nurse Ethel Evans promising to keep a lookout and make a signal if she had any news.

'Dad says they've constructed spur lines outside cities to take the trains directly to the military hospitals so they don't go into main railway stations.'

'There's going to be so many.' Rob lowered his voice. 'Yet they're still telling us we are winning the war.'

Kenneth shrugged his shoulders. 'My dad says we shouldn't believe everything we read in the newspapers.'

'What are you two whispering?' The bulk of Jed's shadow fell over the boys.

Rob and Kenneth got to their feet. Jed was bigger and heavier than them, and if it came to a fight there was a good chance he'd beat them both. At break time he amused himself by charging around the yard pulling the girls' hair. Rob had warned Millie: 'Jed's a bully, so best keep out of his way.' Normally Rob and Kenneth avoided the playground if Jed was on one of his rampages.

They hadn't noticed him creeping up beside them.

Rob ignored Jed and spoke directly to Kenneth. 'Let's go to the cloakroom.'

Jed stuck his face up against Rob's. 'Your mum's gone barmy,' he mocked.

Rob's face went red. He pushed his hands into his trouser pockets. Dad's advice had been to always try to talk your way out of a situation rather than get into a fight. But his dad had also said that sometimes you had to stand up for yourself. Jed had insulted his, Rob's, mother. Rob bunched his fists and pulled them out of his pocket. 'Take that back!'

Millie stepped between them. 'Rob, I need my scone. I left it in my desk. I'm too scared to go and get it 'cos we've not to go into the classroom at playtime.' Rob hesitated. 'Please, Rob, I'm hungry.'

'That's right. Off you go. Run along and find your sister's scone.'

Rob made to take a step forward, but Kenneth dragged on his arm. 'If you fight him, you'll get caned. He's not worth it.'

Reluctantly Rob allowed his sister and his friend to pull him away from Jed's taunting voice. He went inside the school and walked quietly along the corridor to Millie's classroom. It was the work of seconds to retrieve the scone from her desk. Rob breathed in relief. It was one of Miss Finlay's pet hates to have children going in and out of the classroom during recess. On his way back Rob saw that his own classroom door was ajar. He wondered who'd had the nerve to disobey their teacher. Rob put his eye to the hinged part of the door where he could see into the classroom through the crack.

Miss Finlay was sitting at her desk, head bowed. Before her lay the crumpled paper of a War Office telegram.

With a sense of shock Rob recalled that one of the names he'd read out this morning on the 'killed in action' list was Sergeant-major Finlay – Miss Finlay's father.

Rob returned to where Millie was standing with her friends around the big metal stove the janitor fired up on cold days. They'd placed their tin mugs full of water to heat on the top. One of the girls dropped a blob of jam from her bread into the mug to flavour the water and the rest copied her. They compared flavours and swapped cups. Kate Ward, who was in his class, smiled at him. Rob looked away. Ward had been another of the names on the list outside the post office.

In the afternoon session Kate Ward's mother and several other mothers and grandmothers came and took children home from the school early. Their surnames echoed in Rob's head as Miss Finlay called them out of class – the same names he'd read from the casualty list.

Although their teacher had permitted painting or silent reading, the atmosphere in the classroom became gloomy. Even Jed was quiet. Miss Finlay made no comment when he laid his head on his desk and fell asleep.

On the way home from school Millie put her hand in Rob's. Since she'd turned seven she rarely took his hand, but after the War Office telegram had arrived she had gone back to doing this.

'Soldiers will shoot at the messenger dogs when they're

running across the battlefields,' she said. 'They'll try to stop the dog delivering their message, won't they?'

Rob remembered what Nurse Evans had said about battlefield conditions. He felt sick in his stomach at the thought of the dogs and the horses in the mud.

Millie was trying to be brave. 'I suppose I shouldn't make a fuss if it is going to make us win the war. I suppose the war will be over sooner if the dogs help. Maybe our puppies will be sent to where Daddy is. Maybe Daddy will see them or hear them barking and recognize them as Nell's puppies. But I don't think they should be allowed to take the baby pup.'

Rob was only half listening as Millie chatted on.

'I know you let me have the puppy 'cos it was the littlest. And I'm the littlest in our family. And he was quite feeble for the first few days. But Nell's such a good mummy dog she gave that puppy special care. That's why he's alive.'

'And also because you looked after him,' Rob said.

Millie smiled her thanks at his praise.

'Of course you did,' he went on stoutly. 'You were very caring when he was born.'

'It does seem a bit daft to have saved his life and then he gets sent to the war. But I suppose we must all make sacrifices.'

Millie was repeating something she'd heard an adult say, Rob thought. 'If it hadn't been for you he wouldn't have made it. The runt of a litter often dies.'

Suddenly he stopped in the middle of the road.

'What is it?' Millie asked him.

'Let's get home as fast as we can,' said Rob. 'I've had a brilliant idea.'

CHAPTER TWELVE

'One of Nell's puppies has died?'

'Yes.'

Rob's eyes slid away from his mother's face as he answered her. He found it hard to lie in normal circumstances, but almost impossible to do it to his mother.

'I thought I should tell you. So you'd know that when the Army Procurement Officer comes round to get them, there will be one less.'

'Oh.' His mother's voice sounded distant, even though she was only standing a few feet from him in the kitchen. Since the delivery of the War Office telegram it was as

if, inside her head, she had moved and was living somewhere else.

'It was the one I was going to give to Millie,' Rob went
on. 'It was the smallest pup. The runt. The runt of a litter
often dies.'

'That's true,' his mum said slowly. She looked from Rob
to Millie. 'I'd have thought you'd be more upset.'

'We all have to do our bit,' Millie intoned.

'What?' Their mum looked bewildered.

'A noble sacrifice for the war effort,' Millie said.

'It's just something Millie's heard a grown-up saying, or
read on one of those government posters that Mrs Shelby
has put up in the post office.' Rob flashed his eyes at Millie.
He didn't want his mum to have to think too much about
this. 'We're going to bury it in the back garden.'

'You'll need a box.'

'I'll find one,' Rob said quickly. 'There's no need for
you to bother. Can you remember to say to the Army
Procurement Officer when he comes that one of Nell's

pups died?' He patted his mother's hand. 'You go and lie down for a bit. I'll leave Nell with you while Millie and I take care of everything that needs doing.'

Rob waited until his mother had gone into her bedroom and closed the door before he went to the outhouse.

'What are you doing?' Millie asked as he packed wood, straw, nails, hacksaw, hammer, chicken wire and a host of other items into a large haversack. Then he picked up Millie's pup and stowed him inside his jacket.

'These things are going to help me deal with your puppy. Fill one of the small churns with water from the stand pipe in the yard and you can carry that.'

'Where are we taking him?' Millie gasped out the question as they ran from their cottage towards the hills.

'There's a big old house in the woods in the valley below Glebe Farm,' Rob replied. 'Mill House – the owners shut it up and moved somewhere else when their only son was killed at the beginning of the war.'

'We can't go there.' Millie stopped. 'It's haunted. Everyone knows that.'

'Because people say it's haunted doesn't mean it actually is. It's mainly Jed that says things like that 'cos he lives over that way. He's always trying to scare or annoy people.'

'It's not only Jed that says it,' said Millie. 'I've heard Mrs Shelby tell stories about the ghost of a dead soldier. The ghost soldier walks in his pale white shroud, sobbing and sighing, through the attic rooms of the house because that's where his nursery was when he was a baby. She says she saw him when she and Annie were in the woods picking blue-bells in the spring, so I know it's true.'

'That's one of those tall tales people tell. You don't believe in elves or brownies or fairies any more, do you?'

'No-o,' said Millie.

Rob thought it likely that she did still believe in fairies. He'd heard Millie playing with her doll outside and nattering on about fairy rings. He'd seen her setting out flower-petal cups and plates made from leaves to have a tea party for tiny imaginary guests.

'Come on, Millie,' he urged her. 'Forget about ghosts. If we want to save your puppy, we have to get to the woods and home again so that we can dig a pretend grave in our garden before the Army Procurement Officer arrives.' Rob pulled the collar of his jacket higher to hide the pup, who'd pushed his head up from inside to see what was happening.

'We might forget about ghosts,' said Millie, 'but this one doesn't forget about us. Mrs Shelby says the ghost soldier cannot cross over to the other side 'cos he wasn't able to save his friend from dying of his wounds. The spirit of the ghost soldier will not be at peace until he rescues another soldier from death.'

'Then he can help us rescue our puppy,' Rob snapped. 'Are you coming, or aren't you?'

Rob wasn't absolutely sure that there weren't ghosts. But it was daylight and the woods glowed with the colours of late summer. Halloween, when spirits came out to haunt people, was weeks away. He strode off in the direction of Mill House.

'Wait for me!' Millie decided that keeping her puppy safe outweighed any fear of ghosts. She hurried to catch up.

'We need to be careful that nobody sees us.' Rob glanced around before going into the trees. There was no one there. Why then did he feel that someone was watching them? He paused. In addition to his sister's footsteps there was another noise behind him. A soft tread over leaves, the slight scrunch of twigs. An animal? Deer came down from the hills . . . But only in colder weather when they were hungry. A fox maybe, or a badger . . . But those creatures hunted at night. Rob looked back. Dappled sunlight made patterns on the forest floor. The leaves were rustling as squirrels leaped from branch to branch gathering nuts for their winter store. Rob gave his head a shake to clear it of any lingering notions of spooks and spirits. They went on until they came to the high wall that contained the grounds of Mill House. The iron gates leading to the wide driveway of the house were locked shut.

'We'll circle round. There's bound to be a place where we can get over the wall.'

Rob's eyes were drawn to the front of the house – to the attic windows where the ghost was said to be. He started to turn his head to speak to Millie, when—

A flicker of movement.

No blinds or drapes covered the attic windows. With the sun shining directly onto the house it was obvious there was nothing there. Yet Rob was sure he'd seen a blur of white.

'Over here,' Millie called to him. 'There's a tree fallen near to the wall.' The old elm tree must have been blown over during a storm. Its upper branches, brushing against the wall, were strong enough to bear their weight as they hauled themselves to the top.

From this vantage point Rob could see the house and gardens of the estate. Apart from those in the attic, the windows were firmly shuttered, the gardens overgrown and neglected. He realized that he wouldn't be able to force an entry. But in the part of garden farthest from the house, deep among shrubbery, he could see the roof of a garden hut.

'Let's explore there.' He led Millie along the side of the house and down a path that eventually ended in a thicket of trees, followed by dense rhododendrons and then a tangle of thorn bushes. They came to a halt.

'It's like the castle after the Sleeping Beauty had slept for a hundred years,' said Millie.

'Then it's the perfect place to hide your dog,' said Rob. 'No one will ever find him here.'

'We need a magic sword.'

'Or a hacksaw.' Rob opened up the haversack and took out the one he had packed. He went on his hands and knees and cut a tunnel through the bushes until they reached the hut. It was an old potting shed, but the roof and walls were intact. Rob pushed open the door, sending dozens of spiders scuttering away.

'Yeuchh!' said Millie.

'Lend a hand.' Rob issued instructions to his sister to divert her mind from what other beasties might be lurking in the corners. Millie held offcuts of wood while he nailed them together with chicken wire across the front to make a long cage for the puppy. One end he boxed off with a hinged flap, where he scattered the wood shavings. 'You've got to train him to use that area as a toilet,' he told Millie, 'so that he keeps his living area clean.'

Millie hugged him. Rob was glad his face was already red from his exertions so that she didn't see him blush.

'We've still our chores to do,' he said. 'Let's settle the puppy down and go home. We'll visit him in the morning and after school to feed and exercise him and change his water.'

Millie spread straw on the floor of the cage and put the puppy inside. 'Be a good doggie.' She patted him on the head. 'I'll come back and see you soon.'

'You mustn't tell anyone about this,' Rob told her. 'Especially not Pearl and Daisy. They might let it slip to Jed, and if he found out he'd make trouble for us.'

'When do you think we can bring him home?' Millie asked.

'It might not be until the war is finished.'

'When will that be, Rob?' Millie looked at her brother with trusting eyes.

He bent his head to avoid her gaze as he repacked his haversack. His sister was too young for him to tell her the truth. But he didn't want to become one of the people who were telling lies about the war.

'Umm . . .' He searched in his mind for what he could say. 'Maybe we can take him home before the end of the war. Maybe we can say that we found a lost pup in the woods. His colouring is different from Nell's other pups, so people might not suspect he belongs to her. He's got shades of dun in his coat.'

'Oh, so he has!' Rather than being upset that her puppy wasn't purely black and white, Millie was pleased that he was unique. 'He's got patches of light brown – like the beaches at Gullane where we made sandcastles that summer.'

'Yes, like Gullane sands,' Rob agreed. One July day, the month before war broke out, Dad had borrowed Farmer Gordon's horse and cart and they'd gone to the seaside for a treat. Gullane had a long stretch of beach with a vast expanse of golden sand and clumps of grass to shelter in. After that, every night for the whole of the summer holidays, Mum had read *Treasure Island* because Gullane was where Robert Louis Stevenson visited as a child. Rob had played make-believe among the miles of sand dunes, imagining boxes of buried gold and pirate ships sailing in from the sea. Dad had told them that Robert Louis Stevenson had made up his story from his childhood memories.

'The summer before Daddy went away,' said Millie.

Two years ago, and yet she remembered.

'Sandy!' Millie exclaimed. 'That will be my doggie's name! Sandy. Do you like that name, little puppy?'

The pup snuffled happily and licked her hand.

'He *does* like it,' she declared.

'Sandy it is, then,' said Rob.

'It'll not be for too long, anyway,' Millie assured her puppy as she settled him in the straw. 'Daddy said that the war would soon be over.'

Rob didn't say anything as he propped a heavy piece of wood up against the door so that no wild animal could get into the shed to harm the pup. From what he had seen while running through the train yesterday he thought that the war was going to last a whole lot longer than any of them had thought.

As they retraced their steps across the lawn, Millie tried to avoid looking at the house. 'It's creepy when it's getting dark. The windows are like big eyes staring at me.'

'Well, I'm here,' said Rob, 'so there's no need to be scared.' He tried not to dwell on it, but the fading light did make the house and garden a spooky place.

As he helped Millie over the wall, Rob couldn't resist taking a final glance back at the house.

Again – from the end attic window . . . a flash of white.

Rob's breath caught in his throat. Then he laughed at himself. It would be a gull nesting on the windowsill. Not a ghost.

There were no such things as ghosts.

CHAPTER THIRTEEN

The very next afternoon the Army Procurement Officer came to the cottage.

Rob and Millie had coaxed their mother out of her room to sit down at the table and drink some tea, when there was a rap on the door. Before Rob could answer it, the door opened and a man in the uniform of an army major stood there.

'Please, no!' Rob's mother let out a scream.

'Calm yourself, woman,' the man said. 'There's nothing to be alarmed about.'

'Are you bringing me bad news?'

'No, I have not come for that purpose,' the major said. 'I want to speak to the man of the house.'

'My father is enlisted in the army,' Rob told him.

'I'm glad to hear that,' the major replied. 'My business here with you is to collect some collie pups.' He held out an envelope to Rob's mother.

'What?' She stood up, leaning on the table.

When she didn't make any move to take the envelope from him, the officer said impatiently, 'This contains my authorization and a slip for you to fill in. You'll be able to collect your compensation money at the post office.'

Rob's mother crossed to the range and sat down in the big chair where his father used to sit. She turned her face away and stared into the fire.

The major put the envelope on the kitchen table. 'It's there for you when you're ready to deal with it. Now' – he addressed Rob – 'where are these pups?'

'I'll bring them to you,' Rob offered.

'Me too,' said Millie. 'I'm really good at helping.'

'Just do as you've been asked and show me where they are,' the major said. 'I've got a proper transportation basket for them and they need to be labelled before being packed up.'

Rob glanced at his mother. 'Millie and I are going to take this officer to get Nell's pups. Best if you sit where you are,' he said distinctly. 'I'll leave Nell with you.' He didn't even have to give his dog the order. Nell went to the big chair and put her head on his mother's lap.

'Tidy little place you have here,' the major commented as they went out of the cottage. 'Is your father fighting in France?'

'Yes,' said Rob. He didn't like this man, and decided he wouldn't tell him about the War Office telegram. But it was possible that he knew the movements of his father's regiment, so Rob made an effort to sound friendly. 'My father is in the Border Guards. Have you ever fought beside them?'

'I've never met anyone from the Guards. As a rule I don't see regimental soldiers.'

'What soldiers do you see?' Millie took her lead from Rob and forced a smile.

'Actually, I'm awaiting my posting for active service. At the present I'm based in Britain. Training dogs – that's what I do.'

Rob's heart was beating very fast as he led the major to the outhouse. Millie stayed close by him. They stood at the door while the officer went inside.

'You should be proud that your dog's pups have been chosen to help the war effort,' the major told them. 'Communications are vital in a war. Field telephone cables get damaged during bombardment, so information and messages from HQ don't reach front-line commanders. Then soldiers die who might have lived. Dogs can move over terrain where it's impossible for vehicles and horses to travel. A human runner struggling through mud is an easy target for enemy fire. It's harder for the snipers to hit a dog because a well-trained animal is much swifter than a man.'

'I know,' said Rob, thinking of the streak of black and white that was Nell racing ahead of him and his father when corralling the sheep.

'There's a fine dog-training school here in Scotland. That's where your pups will be sent. Don't you want to say goodbye to them?' asked the major.

Millie tightened her grip on Rob's fingers. 'No,' Rob said. 'Thank you.'

The officer lifted every pup individually, examined it, and made notes in a notebook. Then he tagged each one, put a collar round its neck and placed it in a closed basket with wire windows. When he'd finished he counted them, looked at his papers, and counted them again.

'I've come to the right place, haven't I?' he asked. 'The family name is Gowrie, of End Cottage, Glendale village?'

'Yes,' Rob said. 'That's us.'

'There's five puppies listed. I've only got four here.'

'One died.' Rob tried to face the man as he told the lie.

'One died?' The major's eyes narrowed. 'When did it die?'

'The other day.'

'The other day?'

Rob nodded. His face twitched. He could feel his resolve dwindling. Telling someone a direct lie was harder than he thought it would be.

'Would that be after the county vet came by?'

'Yes.' Rob's voice wavered.

'What caused the dog to die?'

Rob felt Millie's nails dig into his arm. For her sake he made his voice stronger. 'I don't know. He just died.'

'I see.' The major swung round and headed back towards the cottage. 'I want to speak to your mother. Will she still be in your house?'

Rob shrugged. It was likely that his mother had gone to lie down on her bed. She'd been doing that a lot since the telegram arrived.

'Mrs Gowrie!' the officer called out.

To Rob's surprise, his mother came from behind the cottage. She hadn't pegged out a washing for weeks. Whatever clothing or sheets she managed to do was left lying in bundles for Rob or Millie to hang up.

'Mrs Gowrie,' the major said briskly, 'the boy is telling me that one of the pups has died. Is this true?'

'Did Rob say it?'

'Yes, but I am asking you . . .'

She put her hand on her son's shoulder. 'My son has

been brought up honestly,' she said. 'I trust him to do what's right.'

'I hope for your sake that this is what has actually happened. Disobeying army orders is treason, you know,' the major said in a hectoring tone.

'Come with me.' Rob's mother led the way to their back garden. She pointed to a mound of earth beside the drying green. 'This is where the children buried their puppy.'

The major knelt down. He examined the newly dug earth and the wooden cross: Rob had burned the name *Sandy* onto it with a red-hot poker. Below the cross was a jam jar filled with fresh flowers.

'Was this the puppy the vet described as having a dun-coloured marking on one ear?' he asked.

Millie burst into tears. 'Sandy was to be my dog,' she sobbed.

'Oh! Oh, all right, then,' the major stumbled. 'There's no need to take on so.'

Millie snivelled and wiped her nose on her sleeve. 'Sandy's gone away and I don't have a puppy dog.'

Rob spoke up. 'I gave him to her because he was the smallest puppy, quite poorly.'

'Ah, the runt!' the major said. 'Runts often die. The mother dog rejects them and won't allow them to feed from her.'

Rob clenched his jaw. How dare this man suggest that Nell would treat one of her young like that! She'd given that pup special attention. Obviously she'd been shut up in the house by his mother, otherwise this man would see how his dog would react to having her pups taken away.

The major put out his hand and patted Millie on the head. 'There, there. Don't fret. The dam will have more pups one day, I'm sure.'

'But I want a puppy now.' Millie put her hands over her face and began to cry in earnest.

'I'll be on my way.' The major hurriedly picked up the basket and marched off down the lane to where his truck was parked.

Millie spread her fingers and watched him go.

'Good for you, Millie, pretending to cry at the right

moment,' Rob said when the major had gone and his mother was back inside their cottage. 'I didn't realize you could turn on tears like that. You could be an actress on the stage when you grow up.'

'I wasn't pretending,' Millie said. 'I was crying 'cos I thought he was going to dig up the earth and open the box with the big stone in it.'

'Ssshhhh!' Rob put his finger to his lips. 'No one must know. You understand? Not even Mummy.'

Millie nodded.

'And it was clever of you to put the jar of flowers on the grave. That made it more convincing.'

'It wasn't me who put the flowers there,' said Millie. 'I thought it was you.'

In the kitchen Rob's mother was listlessly stirring soup in a pot on the range. Rob looked at her. She had grown thin, and was barely able to concentrate on one thing at a time. Yet . . . if Millie hadn't put the flowers on the grave and he hadn't done it, that left only one other person in the house.

Rob noticed the bundle of wet clothes lying in the tub by the mangle. There had been no clothes on the washing lines outside, yet his mother had been in the back garden. So it must have been her who'd cut flowers for the jam jar. Rob felt a pang of guilt: his mother believed that the puppy had died. Had it made her think that perhaps Dad too was dead? And, having no grave to stand beside to mourn him, had she decided to place flowers there in his memory?

CHAPTER FOURTEEN

R ob waited until it was almost dark before going to visit Sandy at Mill House.

He told his mother that he would check on the hens and the other livestock. After a minute or so he went back into the cottage to say that one of the hens must have got out.

'I'll take Nell and Millie with me and we'll look for it,' he said. 'We might be gone for a bit. Maybe as far as the woods. We don't want a fox getting her.'

His mother was washing up the dishes at the sink. She nodded vaguely.

Rob picked up the storm lantern, and he and his sister ran as fast as they could towards the hills.

'We won't stay long,' Rob told Millie. He guessed that by this time the Army Procurement Officer would be well out of their area. But even though he was sure they had fooled the major into believing one of Nell's pups had died, Rob was apprehensive. Supposing he found out they'd lied to him? There would be the most almighty row. He must make sure the puppy stayed well hidden.

Millie shivered as they entered the wood. 'There are faces on the tree trunks,' she said. 'The wood sprites are watching us.'

'Nobody's watching us,' Rob said with more certainty than he felt. 'Wood sprites don't exist.'

'Yes they do,' Millie said. 'But that's all right, 'cos wood sprites are benign creatures and will guard us on our way.'

'You're in the village post office far too often listening to Mrs Shelby's stories.'

'You do it too, Rob,' Millie accused him. 'Ever since the telegram arrived you make excuses to go in to hear what Mrs Shelby's saying about the war.'

'She always reads bits out of the newspapers,' said Rob.

'I'm hoping one day she'll mention the Border Guards. It was useful to be there last week, otherwise I wouldn't have known about the hospital trains. That's what made me ask Kenneth about them. Then he asked his dad, who told him the day and the time it was due to pass this way. Now we've got Nurse Evans helping us too.'

They walked for another minute before Millie spoke. 'But if Nurse Evans *does* find Daddy on one of the hospital trains, then . . .' She paused. 'Rob, the soldiers on the hospital trains are very, very sick.'

'We'd know where he was, though, and even if he's wounded, he'd be able to write to us again.'

'Supposing he's lost an arm and can't write?'

'Someone would do it for him, like Nurse Evans or Bert, or maybe even Captain Morrison.'

'But not Chesney,' Millie said.

'Definitely not Chesney,' Rob agreed. He mimicked Chesney shouting at him. '*You! Farm boy. Out of here. At once!*'

Millie giggled. There was a silence, and then she said, 'But supposing Daddy got a bump on the head and doesn't remember his address? Supposing he doesn't remember who he is?'

'They'll know which regiment he's from by his uniform and his cap badge.'

'Supposing his cap came off and got lost?'

'All soldiers wear a tag around their neck which identifies them.'

'But supposing—'

'Millie!'

His sister lapsed into silence. Then her hand crept into his. Rob looked down at her curly head bobbing along beside him. 'He'll be all right,' he reassured her. 'Really, Millie, we'll just have to wait it out. Dad will come home. And I've thought of another way to get more information. I'm going to go to the Otterby farm to ask which hospital Jack's been sent to. When we know that, we can go and visit him and take Nell with us. Jack likes Nell, and he might be able to talk more when she's there and tell us what happened to the regiment.'

'You always have good plans, Rob,' Millie said. 'It was

clever of you to pretend my puppy had died and then think of hiding him here. I'm lucky to have a big brother like you. I feel sorry for Pearl and Daisy. They've got Jed for a big brother, and he isn't nice at all.'

They reached Mill House and went down the path towards the potting shed. Nell stopped at the entrance to the tunnel through the thorn bushes and gave a short sharp bark.

'Quiet,' Rob said. 'I know you're excited to see your pup, but we need you to be quiet.' They were far enough away from Glebe Farm not to be heard, but there might be poachers in the woods looking for a rabbit or even a deer.

Millie pushed on eagerly. Stepping over a piece of wood, she opened the door and went in. Rob lit the lamp as Millie took Sandy out of his cage. Nell began licking her pup and pushing him with her nose. Rob let Millie feed him some leftovers they'd sneaked from their kitchen while he gathered up the old straw and soiled wood shavings.

'What was that?' said Millie, turning round.

'What?' Rob was putting down fresh straw and changing the water in the dish.

Millie was looking towards the door.

Nell bristled, the hairs on the back of her neck standing straight up.

'There it is again,' said Millie, and this time Rob heard it too. A scuffling – too big for a vole or weasel.

'I told you there was a ghost,' she whispered in fright.

'It's only the wind in the trees.' Rob pointed to the window. 'See? The branches of that bush are tapping against the glass.'

'If it's the ghost soldier walking, then maybe he'll be kind and look after Sandy,' said Millie.

'There's no such thing as ghosts,' Rob said, 'but it's time to go home anyway.'

As he propped the piece of wood against the door to secure it, something occurred to him. He looked at the plank in his hand. When they'd arrived, Millie had been ahead of him. She'd had to step over it . . . it had being lying on the ground – the same piece of wood he'd used to bar the door when they'd brought the pup to the shed. Over the last day and night the wind hadn't been strong enough to dislodge the plank. Rob saw that Nell's tail was up, her ears forward; she was casting about. If the noise they'd heard was only the wind, why then was she on alert?

Had someone been inside the shed?

Were they still around, spying on them?

Rob called Nell to him. 'Come here, girl. Stay by Millie,' he commanded. 'Stay close.'

His dog understood his intention. While he took hold of one of his sister's hands, Nell went to her other side. With Millie guarded between them, they made their way through the trees. Rob steadfastly refused to look at the front of the house.

When they were clear of the wood and safely on the pasture land Rob glanced back. There was nothing to be seen. No figure following behind. Nobody spying on them. Only the movement of lengthening shadows as the sun set, a fiery ball in the sky.

CHAPTER FIFTEEN

Early next morning Rob ran to Glebe Farm to refill their milk churn.

'No more hospital trains have been through.' Farmer Gordon winked at him. 'I know you're on the lookout for them so I'm keeping my eyes open too.'

'Kenneth's dad works on the railways,' Rob told him, 'and he said he'd tip us off when the next one's due.'

'That's the type of friend that's handy to have. Although . . . it bears fruit to remember that friends come in all sorts of shapes and sizes.' Mr Gordon's gaze took in the manure pile where Jed was raking the muck into heaps.

Jed? Rob looked at the farmer. He surely couldn't mean

that Jed might be a friend . . . Jed wasn't friendly to anyone. He was a big bully, and everyone stayed away from him.

'There's been railway workers busy down in the valley,' Farmer Gordon went on. 'Come and I'll show you.'

As the farmer walked out of the farm gate, Jed made a rude gesture behind his back. Typical of him to do something like that, Rob thought. Jed wasn't even grateful to the Gordons for the agreement they'd made with his mother. Jed's dad had died in a farm accident, but his mother lived on rent-free in one of the farm workers' cottages as long as Jed worked a certain number of hours on the farm. There were six in his family, and Jed was the eldest at home as his elder sister was a maid in service in Edinburgh. But Mr and Mrs Gordon arranged Jed's work time so that he could still go to school and get an education. Seeing Rob's disapproving look, Jed stuck out his tongue, pointed at him and then made donkey ears by flapping his hands on top of his head. When Nell stopped and took a step towards him, Jed hurriedly picked up the shovel he'd thrown down. Rob stuck out his own tongue at Jed and then whistled to his dog to follow on after him.

'They've almost finished constructing a water tank alongside the track,' Mr Gordon said.

From the top of the hill Rob could see the tank with its hose in place. His spirits lifted. This meant that there would definitely be more trains, and they would all stop in the valley to take on water. Rob wished with all his heart and soul that on one of these trains there would be someone who could give him news about his father.

Millie was already waiting for him when he got back with the milk. She put her finger to her lips. 'Mummy's still sleeping. I filled the water bottle and the bag with straw and food for Sandy.'

'Good girl. You really are growing up, Millie.'

Basking in his praise, his sister skipped ahead of him to the house in the woods. Their visit that morning was rushed, but Rob had enough time to notice that the piece of wood was across the door, in the position where he'd placed it the night before. Perhaps it had been an animal that had disturbed it the previous time . . . or maybe whoever had moved it was taking more care in how they replaced it . . .

Later, in school, Rob was labouring over a page of hard sums when the school janitor opened the classroom door.

'Begging your pardon, Miss Finlay, but there's a gentleman here who wishes to speak to you.'

The children stopped working.

'Mr Ronald!' Miss Finlay spoke severely. 'I am attempting to teach these children long division. You shouldn't interrupt me in the middle of a lesson.'

'The gentleman is an army officer, and what with there being a war on, I thought . . .' Mr Ronald stepped aside as a tall man in British Army uniform entered the classroom.

He marched over to Miss Finlay's desk and executed a full military salute. 'Lieutenant Polden, at your service. Please excuse the intrusion, ma'am. I came to ask permission to use some of the school facilities. I'll wait for the end of the lesson before speaking to you.'

Miss Finlay dropped the stick of chalk she was holding and her face went pink. 'I – I—' she stammered.

It was the first time Rob had ever seen his teacher lost for words.

The officer saluted again, turned on his heel and made for the door.

'Wait!' Miss Finlay called after him. 'Do please speak to me if you wish. I didn't appreciate the importance of the interruption. It's ... it's ... well, arithmetic is needed in every walk of life, and the children have to be educated, and ...'

'Absolutely true,' Lieutenant Polden agreed. He faced the class. 'Boys and girls! Pay attention to your teacher. Arithmetic is very important. If you can't count, you can't do anything. Your country needs young men and women who can add up a column of figures. How would I know how many men I had if I couldn't count them?' he demanded. 'Arithmetic is a good thing to learn, isn't it?'

'Yes, sir!' Rob and his classmates chorused.

The lieutenant picked up the chalk Miss Finlay had dropped and handed it to her. 'I'll leave you to carry on your work here. Perhaps I could have a word with you at lunch time?' And he strode out of the classroom.

'Er . . .' Miss Finlay looked at the blackboard as if she didn't actually recognize what it was. 'Er . . . that's right,' she said to the class. 'Do as the officer says. Carry on with your work. I'll go and have a word with Lieutenant Polden while you do the rest of your sums. No talking while I'm gone,' she added as she left the room.

'Did you see? He had a medal on his chest.'

'It was the Victoria Cross!'

Rob and his friends were whispering as soon as the door closed behind their teacher.

'There was a pistol at his belt.'

'He's a lieutenant. They always carry handguns.'

The girls were giggling at Miss Finlay blushing. 'Do you think she's fallen in love with him?' Kate Ward asked.

'She's *definitely* in love with him,' said her friend, Beth Halliday. 'His face went red too when he saw her. He must have fallen in love with her at first sight.'

'That's rubbish!' said Kenneth. 'Soldiers don't have time for silly things like love. They're too busy fighting a war.'

'Well, I think it would be good if Lieutenant Polden had fallen in love with our teacher,' Kate argued back, her eyes blazing with sudden passion. 'He could comfort Miss Finlay in her sadness at losing her father.'

In a moment of insight Rob glimpsed her grief – Kate's father was one of the recent dead. He nodded in agreement, and was rewarded with a smile.

The class snapped into silence as Miss Finlay opened the door. 'Lieutenant Polden has requested that his men be allowed to use the school facilities while they are in the village today. We're going to cut lessons this morning, and have an early lunch break. Then, in the afternoon, we will go to the park and see the soldiers on parade.'

CHAPTER SIXTEEN

'**A** tten*shun*!'

'Right turn!'

'Forward march!'

Instead of keeping to the usual straggling line when out on a nature ramble, the boys had formed themselves into ranks to parade through the village to the park. Miss Finlay let them march ahead, shouting out military drill commands to each other. When they arrived in the park, they swarmed among the army tables and tents.

Straw men dressed in German Army uniforms were hanging from some of the trees. The soldiers invited anyone passing to have a go at charging the enemy. Jed was first to grab the rifle with bayonet attached.

'Get a grip on that, son. You stick him good and proper.'

Jed lunged at the straw man with such force that the blade of the bayonet ripped open the cloth tunic.

'Well done!' The soldier pulled a handful of straw out of the slashed opening and threw it down on the grass. 'Let his blood and guts run out. And if he squeals for mercy, don't you listen to him. Finish him off.' He took the bayonet from Jed and plunged it into the neck of the straw man. 'Like this!'

Rob's stomach contracted. He put his hands to his mouth to hold in the sick rising in his throat.

'How old are you, boy?' he heard the soldier ask Jed.

'Nearly thirteen. But I look older.'

'You do, my son. You definitely do. You're a big lad. And the army needs big brave lads like you.' He tapped the side of his nose. 'The recruiting wagon will be here soon. When it comes along, you add a few years onto your age. Before you know it, you'll have your uniform and your own gun and be ready to fight for King and Country.'

Jed marched off, his chest puffed out with pride.

The paved area round the bandstand had been cordoned off for demonstrations of parade ground drilling. Most of Rob's classmates rooted around in the bushes to find sticks to serve as guns so that they could copy the marching formations. Rob and Kenneth made for the place where Lieutenant Polden was supervising soldiers digging a trench.

'It's got to be a certain shape,' the lieutenant told the boys. 'It's dug in a zigzag pattern for a special reason. If the enemy manage to get through the wire and into a trench to fire at us, we can hide round the corner. If they throw one of their stick grenades, then the blast won't go all the way down the trench, as it would if the trench was a straight line.'

'Do *we* have stick grenades?' asked Kenneth.

'We've got our Mills bombs, which soldiers carry on their belts. But our lads fight hard to discourage them from coming a-calling,' Lieutenant Polden said staunchly. 'The British Army holds the line.'

He let the boys into the trench so that they could be

soldiers holding the line. Rob wondered if that was what his dad had been doing before he went missing – 'holding the line'.

The soldiers set up box periscopes so that the villagers could stand on the fire step and look out into no-man's-land without being seen. Rob could see the schoolhouse and the post office. But that's not what his dad would be seeing. On the hospital train Jack had mentioned barbed wire and land mines.

'How do the soldiers make an advance?' Rob asked.

'Oh, it's a big excitement. The men are fighting fit, every one prepared to do his duty. The rum ration is doled out. The whistle blows. Up the ladder and off we go!'

'Aren't they waiting for us with their guns ready?'

'Our artillery at the rear will have been lobbing shells over our heads at their positions for days ahead of any advance. That softens them up for us to go forward and sort out any that are still lurking there.'

'What if they've been hiding? What if—'

'Excuse me.' Lieutenant Polden had seen Miss Finlay

standing at the mess tent with a group of her girl pupils. 'I think I might go and discuss army cooking with your teacher.'

Rob doubted whether he was really interested in cooking – it was just a pretence so that he could chat to Miss Finlay. Once that happened he wouldn't be able to ask the lieutenant any more questions. But Rob had reckoned without Millie, who'd seen him with the lieutenant and come to join him. She followed as they walked towards the mess tent. 'Our dad is missing. Nobody knows where he is. We're worried about him.'

'Try not to worry. Lots of men go missing in war. It doesn't always mean that they've been killed.'

Rob felt his heart lift. Usually people shook their head when they heard that his mother had been sent a telegram by the War Office.

'Would you know where our dad could be?' Millie asked.

'Do you know the name of his regiment? What battalion? His last posting?'

Lieutenant Polden was surprised and pleased to find

that Rob could recite all the details. 'Your pupil is very knowledgeable,' he said as he approached Miss Finlay.

'Rob's granddad was in the army,' she said. 'His family has a proud tradition of soldiering.'

'I'll try to find out any information I can,' said Lieutenant Polden. 'It will give me an opportunity to come by this way again' – he glanced at Miss Finlay – 'I'm happy to say.'

Millie nudged Rob as Miss Finlay's face turned pink again.

Outside the mess tent, huge pots of food were simmering over braziers. The children and villagers lined up to sample 'battle rations', with the soldiers ladling out plates of stew.

'I wish Mummy was here,' said Millie. 'The lovely smell of the food might have made her eat something.'

Miss Finlay glanced at Millie and at Jed, who was now on his third plateful of stew and potatoes.

She murmured something to Lieutenant Polden, who beckoned to Rob and Jed. 'We always give out rations to our most promising recruits at the end of the day.' He handed them each a bag containing tins of milk and bully beef. Rob noticed that Jed got the bigger bag. Jed was often disruptive in class, getting up from his seat and not doing what he was told; Miss Finlay frequently sent him to stand in the corridor for ten minutes. Yet his bag had more tins in it than Rob's. Sometimes Rob couldn't understand the way adults' minds worked.

Lieutenant Polden removed the cordon from the makeshift parade ground so that the soldiers could march around the village. Off they went, through the park, past the church and post office, round the schoolhouse and back again.

Rob saw a woman coming from the post office. As the marching ranks of men came down the street towards her, she put her shawl over her head, took her young children by the hand, and hurried away. It was Kate's mother. Rob remembered that her husband's name was one of the ones he had called out from the casualty list.

The soldiers began to sing:

'It's a long way to Tipperary, it's a long way to go . . .'

Rob knew it was meant to be a cheerful marching song, but suddenly it seemed terribly sad.

In the darkening evening the flames of the fires sent sparks into the sky. The moon was rising – a harvest moon. His dad was somewhere under the same sky and the same moon. Rob wondered if he was thinking of them and how they might be coping with him not at home.

Miss Finlay was beside Lieutenant Polden. Her head was on a level with his shoulder and she was looking up into his face to hear what he was saying. Rob had seen that expression before. The day his father had left to go to war, they'd stood in the front yard waving him off. He'd kissed Rob's mother and Millie over and over. He'd shaken Rob's hand firmly, but then, impulsively, pulled him towards him in a fierce hug. As his father reached the end of the lane, his mother had run after him. Brimming with love, she'd turned her face up to his for one last kiss. Maybe the girls were right. Maybe Miss Finlay was falling in love with Lieutenant Polden.

Rob moved on. He called to Millie that it was almost time to go home. Then he saw an officer's dugout with a desk and a map spread out on it. It showed Britain and France and Belgium and Germany. Millie caught sight of Pearl and Daisy in the crowds and ran off to play with them. Rob went inside the dugout to examine the map. He traced his finger all the way down through England and across the Channel to France. Where was his dad? Would he ever see him again?

If the Germans had advanced, his dad might have been captured. Rob hoped that the German soldiers would be nice to him. If he hadn't been captured, perhaps he'd been in a British advance and got trapped behind the German line? Maybe, even now, he was trying to escape and make his way back to his base? France and Germany were so big compared to Britain. Someone could easily get lost, especially if the land was churned up with hundreds of bombs and shells exploding. But his dad was very experienced at travelling through the countryside in the worst of conditions. One of

Rob's earliest memories was of being out on the hills with him when unexpected bad weather closed in. His dad had scooped him up and carried him home, cooried in under his shepherd's plaid, snug against the winter storm. It was to him the sheep farmers came if the weather was bad and ewes went missing during lambing season. His dad was the shepherd who could go with Nell through a blizzard in the dark, find the new-born lambs, dig them out of deep snow and bring them home safe.

Would he be able to bring *himself* home safely?

Rob jumped as someone placed their hand on his shoulder. He looked up. Miss Finlay was smiling down at him.

'I'm sure Lieutenant Polden will keep his promise to make enquiries about the movements of the Border Guards over the last months,' she said. 'Try to hold on – a little hope is all that's needed.'

CHAPTER SEVENTEEN

B ut when the next train stopped in Glebe Valley, Rob found it hard to hold onto hope.

He and Millie had arrived early, and as the train approached, Rob saw that the engine was pulling more carriages than the previous one. Farmer Gordon had come down to lend a hand and make sure there was enough water in the new tank. The engine driver and fireman were working fast, so Rob knew he didn't have much time to get all the way along the train. Their manner was different this time. They kept their heads bent and seemed reluctant to chat.

Millie had loaded her basket with sandwiches wrapped in brown paper, which she wanted to give to the medical orderlies for distribution to the wounded soldiers. Rob left her at the water tank with strict instructions not to move from there, then ran down the line. As he went, he called out, 'Nurse Evans? It's Rob – Rob from the farm. Are you there?'

In the centre of the train Rob noticed that there was a carriage with windows of frosted glass. What was going on in there that had to be kept private?

Nurse Evans popped her head out of one of the doors and spoke rapidly. 'No news,' she told Rob. 'I'm sorry. No news.'

'What's the special carriage for?' Rob asked her.

'Surgery,' she replied. 'We've set up an operating theatre on the train. It's for emergency cases.'

Her apron was marked with fresh blood, stained as red as the cape she wore. If the men were emergency cases, why not keep them in France? Or operate on them during the Channel crossing? Maybe there weren't enough military doctors there. Weren't there more in Folkestone or Southampton? Why wait to operate on soldiers on a moving train?

'Please go home now. We're very busy.'

'You won't forget about my dad, will you?'

Nurse Evans managed a smile. 'I won't forget. Off you go.' Before she turned to go inside, Rob thought he saw her brush a tear from her cheek.

As he returned to Millie, he could hear sounds he'd missed when running along the line. Men were moaning and calling for morphine. Coming up to the water tank, he caught part of the conversation the fireman was having with Mr Gordon. '. . . The big pushes don't get us very far. They seem to have more advanced weapons. I don't understand that. Time was, the British Army could outgun and outfight the world.'

'Dad's not on this train,' Rob told Millie.

She was crestfallen, but said, 'I'll give my sandwiches to the engine driver to pass on to Nurse Evans.' She looked around. 'No one else has got off the train.'

Rob reckoned the medical orderlies – indeed, all the staff – would have their hands full dealing with the wounded. 'Good idea,' he said. 'You do that, and then we'll go.' He wanted to leave before Millie heard the terrible groans coming from the men on this train.

'You may keep a sandwich for yourself,' Millie told the driver, who appeared to have forgiven them for getting on his train on the previous occasion. 'Will you keep a lookout for my dad?'

'Millie,' he said as he took the parcels from her, 'every train driver in Britain is keeping a lookout for your dad.'

On Sunday Rob told his mother that he'd take Millie berrying for raspberries and brambles. First they visited Sandy. Millie had brought a length of thick string to use as a lead so that he wouldn't run away when she took him outside to exercise. Afterwards they had put him back, and instead of spending the rest of the day picking berries, they walked three miles across the fields to the Otterby farm.

'Listen, Millie,' Rob said to his sister as they went up the farm lane, 'we must be very careful what we say to Mr and Mrs Otterby. Remember we're not supposed to let anyone know that we were on the train. And we shouldn't tell them that Jack is sick in his head.'

'But we have to let them know that he's going to be in a hospital in Edinburgh. Maybe they don't even know that he's alive.'

Rob thought for a moment. 'We could say he waved to us from the window and we recognized him.'

'Yes, that's a good idea.'

'But we'll only say that if we have to. Hopefully they'll tell us their news without us having to mention the hospital train.'

Rob knocked on the door of the farmhouse. It was opened by Mrs Otterby. He had his speech prepared:

'I hope you don't mind us calling by. You might not know us – we are Rob and Millie Gowrie from Glendale village. We live in End Cottage over the hill from Glebe Farm.'

'Of course I know you! And if I didn't recognize you, then I'd know Nell – the best sheepdog in the county. Look, Mr Otterby . . .' Mrs Otterby addressed her husband. 'It's Millie and Rob Gowrie, and they've got Nell with them.'

Mr Otterby, who was mending boots by the fire, raised his hand in greeting. Mrs Otterby did the talking for two.

'I'm sure I've something you would like to eat.' She lifted the lid of a cake tin. 'Ah, I thought so.' The smell of home baking and icing wafted through the room. 'Take a seat at the table and I'll cut you a slice. It won't compare with your mother's, though. Her cakes are always in high demand at the county fair.'

Rob was glad Millie's mouth was full of cake. Their mother hadn't baked anything but bread in the last weeks. But news travels fast, and bad news travels fastest, so he wasn't too taken aback when Mrs Otterby said tentatively, 'Your dad went to the war, didn't he?'

'Yes,' Rob said, adding, 'Like your son, Jack.'

'I heard your mother's been poorly after getting one of those "missing in action" telegrams. Well, tell her not to take on so. We got one too, but now we've been told that Jack is on his way home.'

'We know,' said Millie.

'You do?' Mrs Otterby said in surprise.

Millie nodded. 'That's why we came to see you.'

'It beats me how you knew,' said Mrs Otterby, 'because we only got word last night.' She reached up and took down a letter which was propped up against the clock on the mantelpiece.

'We saw him.' The words were out of Millie's mouth before Rob could stop her.

'You saw him? Mercy me! You saw our Jack?' Mrs Otterby sat down heavily on a chair.

'On the hospital train, when we—' Millie stopped, realizing she was talking too much. 'I mean, we think we saw him. That is, it looked like him.'

'Where? Where did you see him?'

Mr Otterby paused in the act of hammering a seg onto the sole of his boot.

Millie pressed her lips together. She gave Rob an agonized look.

'Um' – Rob fumbled for a suitable story – 'we were getting our milk from Glebe Farm the other morning, and a hospital train went by on its way to Edinburgh. Full of soldiers, it was, and . . . and someone waved to us from the train. And it looked like Jack.'

'Oh my,' said Mrs Otterby. She addressed her husband. 'Did you hear that, dear? Jack waved to the children from the train. Now that's a hopeful sign, isn't it?'

'What did he say in his letter?' Rob asked. 'Did he say where he'd been in France? Does he mention what was happening with the regiment?'

'Has he seen our daddy?' Millie chimed in. 'Would he know where he is?'

'Oh, children!' Mrs Otterby laughed and held up her hand. 'He didn't actually write the letter himself.' She glanced at her husband. He bent his head and continued re-soling his boot. 'But Jack's alive and all of a piece, and I'm happy for that at least.' She looked at her husband again. His gaze remained on his work.

'Could we go and visit him please?' Rob asked. 'We could chat for a bit and maybe he could tell us something – anything – about the Border Guards.'

'We've been told no visiting allowed. Not until he's a bit better. He's got' – she hesitated – 'a long road of recovery ahead of him.'

Mr Otterby got up and went outside.

'Why not?' asked Millie. 'Chatting is good for sick soldiers. Nurse Evans said— Ow!'

Underneath the table Rob kicked his sister quite hard on the leg.

'Nurse Evans?' Mrs Otterby looked from Rob to Millie and back again.

Rob stood up. 'We have to go. Thank you for the cake.'

Mr Otterby was standing at the farm gate looking out over the fields. He whistled to his own sheepdogs, tipped his cap to Rob, and then walked away towards the hills. Nell looked longingly after him, as though she too wanted to be roaming free. Rob clicked his fingers to bring his dog to heel and set off swiftly towards Glendale.

'I'm sorry, Rob.' Millie was jogging to keep up with him. 'I didn't mean to say Nurse Evans's name.'

'You need to learn to keep your mouth shut! If you blab

what we know to everybody we meet, then the army will find out and put a big fence along the railway track and we'll never get to speak to Nurse Evans again.'

'I'm really, really sorry.' Millie was crying. 'I'll never do it again. It was just that Mrs Otterby is so keen for news, like us. And . . . and Mr Otterby seems embarrassed about Jack.'

Rob couldn't stay angry at his sister for long. And he'd noticed Mr Otterby's manner too. 'Maybe he's ashamed that Jack isn't wounded in the regular way. It's not so honourable to be hurt in the head.'

'Why?'

'It could look like Jack was being cowardly. Like he didn't want to fight. When people are hurt on their body, they get sympathy, but if there's something wrong inside their head, then they get laughed at, or mocked.'

'Why is that?'

Rob shrugged. 'I don't know. It's harder for a doctor to heal the inside sickness. And the person can't seem to help themselves.'

'Like Mummy.' Millie's voice was barely a whisper.

* * *

Before going home Rob and Millie went to check on Sandy again. Rob studied the bar of wood before removing it to go into the shed. It wasn't quite in the same place. So either an animal or a human being had disturbed it. It couldn't have been a ghost who had done it. Ghosts didn't have to open doors. They could glide through.

Millie took the puppy outside, tethered him to a bush and let him scamper around.

Nell was restless. Pacing, and sniffing in corners. She gazed at Rob as if trying to tell him something.

'Have you picked up a scent? What is it?' Rob put his mouth close to Nell's ear so that his sister wouldn't hear. But she was playing with her puppy in the clearing around the hut and chatting to him nonstop, too preoccupied to be listening in.

Rob was on edge. After five minutes he said to Millie, 'Put Sandy back in his cage and let's go home. We've been away from Mummy long enough today.'

They left, crawling through the tunnel into the

rhododendrons, and then made their way through the trees to the path, when—

A shadow! By a silver birch, taller than any woodland creature, a figure approached. Nell bristled. Rob signalled to Millie and they concealed themselves behind a tree trunk.

The branches parted. A young deer flitted through the trees, pausing to stare at them – its wide eyes two deep pools of darkness. Rob's heart was banging in his chest. They were about to continue along the path when Nell growled and went on alert, taking a stance in front of Rob and Millie.

Then they both heard the noise of an engine. It was a lorry coming up the main avenue. Gravel sputtered from beneath its tyres as it stopped. Millie squeezed herself close to her brother.

'There's nothing to be scared of,' said Rob. 'Wait here with Nell while I go and investigate.' He moved softly round the side of the house.

The front door was standing open. Two men were unloading cardboard boxes from a truck and carrying them inside. One was around the age of Rob's father and dressed in a major's uniform. The other was much older, with a beard and spectacles.

They worked in silence. When they'd finished, the older man began a conversation, speaking English with a strong foreign accent. 'We'll bring the rest of the equipment tomorrow and hide it before the medical staff and patients arrive.'

The major nodded. 'This new clinic is the perfect cover for our project.'

The older man took him by the shoulder and spoke urgently. 'Take the utmost care how you manage this. No one – and I mean *no one* – must detect the secret work that I will be doing here.'

Making sure that his feet did not crunch on the gravel, Rob backed away from the door.

'What's happening?' Millie asked him as he led her towards the wall, the wood and home.

'There were two men taking boxes from the truck into Mill House. They talked about setting up a clinic for wounded soldiers, but then they said something else.'

'Who are they? What did they say?'

'I'm not sure. One of them had an unusual accent, so I don't know if I heard properly . . .'

Rob decided that he wouldn't tell Millie that the army might be planning to use Mill House as a secret head-quarters. It was enough that she had to keep quiet about the hidden puppy. Tomorrow at school he could ask Kenneth if his dad had heard anything.

CHAPTER EIGHTEEN

As often happened in Glendale village, it was the postmistress, Mrs Shelby, who was first with the information.

'Mill House is to be converted into a convalescent home for wounded soldiers,' she announced to her morning customers. Rob manoeuvred himself nearer.

'It will be officers only,' someone said.

'I've heard it's for ordinary soldiers' – Mrs Shelby gave her audience a significant look – 'but it's for *special* cases, if you understand my meaning.'

Rob didn't understand. Did Mrs Shelby mean that it was for soldiers who were dying? When he got to school, he found that Kenneth had more details.

'My dad says that they're going to convert Mill House into a nursing clinic, but not for the physically wounded. It's for those whose nerves have gone. They're supposed to shake so much they can't hold a gun to fire it. I don't believe that shell shock is a real illness,' Kenneth added. 'I mean, you'd shake a lot if you were really frightened that you were going to die, wouldn't you? That's normal.'

'I'm not sure . . .' Rob chewed his lip. He couldn't say anything about the incident on the hospital train. But after meeting Private Ames and Jack Otterby, he definitely did believe that shell shock was a real illness.

'It's not a reason to be sent home,' Kenneth went on. 'If everybody who was scared was sent home, then there would be no soldiers left to fight the war.'

Rob longed to discuss the condition of the soldiers on the train with his friend, but he'd given his word to Captain Morrison that he'd remain quiet. The captain was relying on him to do his bit to keep morale high – it was as important to do that on the Home Front as it was on the battlefield, he'd said. And, in return, he'd promised to make it his business to find out about Rob's father. They'd exchanged a proper salute. It was a bond of honour.

'I wonder if the patients will be allowed visitors,' Kenneth went on. 'I'd like to see someone who's supposed to have shell shock.'

'I'll come with you if you like,' Rob offered, thinking it would be a good opportunity to try to find out what secret work was taking place inside Mill House.

'You could take your mum with you when you go, Rob Gowrie . . .' Jed was eavesdropping. 'But they might not let her out again.'

Rob shoved Jed violently. 'You're worried that they'll put *you* in there and throw away the key!'

'I doubt if the doctors at the new clinic will welcome visitors,' Miss Finlay commented when she heard what was happening at Mill House. 'Complete rest and quiet is what's needed for those with nervous debility. I know that it's been common practice to go into the woods to snare a rabbit for the pot. But best to stay out of that area and not encroach on the grounds of the estate.'

'It's haunted anyway,' said Kate Ward.

'There's no such thing as ghosts,' Kenneth scoffed.

'Yes there is,' she insisted. 'Mrs Shelby at the post office has seen the pale face of the ghost soldier in his long white burial shroud. That's why people in the village avoid it.' Several of the girls nodded, agreeing with Kate.

Jed gave Rob a sly look. 'Doesn't stop some folk from sneaking up there, though, does it?'

Rob stared at Jed. What did he mean by that remark?

'Don't mind him,' said Kenneth. 'Come and see what's happening outside.'

Rob went to the window. An army recruiting wagon was drawing up outside the school.

Miss Finlay sighed. 'Another early dismissal for the school, I expect.'

To the disappointment of the pupils, the army officers waited until the end of the school day before setting up their recruiting station in the school hall. Rob and Kenneth dallied to watch them carrying in weighing scales, a height-measuring stick and a screen behind which medical examinations would take place. They offered to help, but the recruiting sergeant wasn't as friendly as Lieutenant Polden.

'Be off out of here!' he told the boys. 'I don't want children hanging around.'

The boys separated, Kenneth heading home towards the centre of the village, and Rob to where Millie was waiting for him to walk up the hill road to their cottage.

'Look, Rob!' said Millie. 'Jed has joined the queue!'

Jed was standing in line at the school entrance behind a few other local lads.

'Good,' said Rob. 'It'll stop him bothering us in the play-ground.'

'But he can't go,' Millie exclaimed. 'He's too young and he's needed at home. How would his mummy manage without him? Our mummy wouldn't get by without you.'

'It's not our business,' said Rob. 'Ask Pearl and Daisy to stop him. He's their big brother.'

'He won't listen to them.'

'Well, there's even less chance that he would listen to us.'

'Miss Finlay could do it.' Millie pointed to where their teacher was entering the baker's shop on the main street. 'You could ask her.'

'It's nothing to do with us.'

'*Please*, Rob,' Millie said. 'Supposing Jed gets shot. Then his name would appear on one of the casualty lists. You might have to read it out to his mummy.'

Without waiting to see if Rob was prepared to speak to Miss Finlay, Millie ran back into the school, where Jed was now first in the line.

She squirmed in beside him and said in a loud voice, 'Jed is still at school.'

Jed elbowed Millie aside. He spoke to the sergeant. 'I only go to school because I'm made to. I'm old enough to leave and I want to join up.'

'Well spoken, young man!' The sergeant pointed to Millie. 'Is this child a relative of yours?'

'No!' said Jed. 'She's just a nosy wee girl.'

Millie was undaunted. 'I don't think his mummy knows

he's doing this,' she said. 'And Farmer Gordon won't, either. Jed works on the Gordon farm before and after school every day to pay rent on the cottage where his family live.'

The sergeant frowned at Millie. 'Go away,' he ordered her. He addressed Jed. 'I take it that your father has passed on?'

Jed nodded.

'Your army pay should cover the rent on the cottage, so you needn't worry on that score. It's a good life, soldiering. Three meals a day. And the money you earn is your own.' The sergeant winked. 'You can treat a girl to an ice cream any day of the week.'

'I want my pay sent to my mother.'

'Rest assured, son – whatever happens, your mother will be better off.'

'Not if she doesn't have Jed,' said Millie. 'Jed is needed to do the work around the house. Who would chop the fire-wood? His twin sisters are too small and his two younger brothers are babies.'

'You get out of here, Millie Gowrie, and leave me alone!' Jed raged at her.

Miss Finlay appeared at the school door. Before she went inside, a woman stepped out from a group that had gathered there.

'Excuse me, miss,' she said, 'but my son Johnny finished his schooling only last year. He wants to go and kill some Germans in revenge for the deaths of his two older brothers. He's my last son. I've asked him not to, but he won't listen to me. Could you say a word, please? I'd be ever so grateful.'

'Me too.' Kate Ward's mother came forward. 'My lad wants to kill the men who killed his father. My husband is dead, and buried where I'll never see his grave. I don't want the same for my eldest son.'

Rob followed his teacher as she walked to the front of the queue in the school hall. She introduced herself to the sergeant and said: 'Conscription is in force in our country, and with it a recognized procedure for issuing call-up papers. May I ask why the army has decided to send recruiting wagons out?'

'That could be classified information,' the sergeant

joked, 'but as you've a pretty face, I'll answer you.'

Miss Finlay did not smile in response.

'Papers go astray, or our lists can be incomplete. We like to give every loyal subject the chance to come forward.'

'Please do not question our loyalty,' Miss Finlay retorted. 'One million loyal subjects came forward in the first months of the war. Glendale village has done its duty. We have already lost nigh on fifty men from our area – fathers, brothers, husbands, sons.'

The sergeant looked her up and down. 'Please leave,' he said. 'You are preventing me from carrying out my official duties. This is men's work. There's no place for a woman here.'

Miss Finlay did not move. 'Don't you think this village has given enough without taking our children? Some of these lads are underage.' She indicated the line of young men waiting to be signed up.

'I tell them the truth,' said the sergeant. 'War is not just for a day and a dinner.'

'Our children see the banners and hear the sound of a

marching band. What do they know of the real truth of a battlefield?'

Rob recalled what Jack Otterby had said about the bombardment failing to destroy the barbed wire and enemy trenches.

'Conditions have improved,' the sergeant stated in what sounded like a rehearsed speech. 'Every soldier is now issued with a steel helmet and the war is entering the last phase. We've got them on the run. It's a time for a man to earn medals and win glory for himself, his family and his village.' He raised his voice. 'Would you have these young men labelled conchie cowards?'

'If by a conchie you mean a conscientious objector, then I do have sympathy with people who stand up for what they believe in and refuse to kill a fellow human being.'

'I thought so – you're one of them!' The sergeant folded his arms smugly. 'But what would your "*conscientious objector*" do if a battalion of Germans marched into this village? Eh? What if they shot all the menfolk, and the women too, and the children, even babies in their cribs?

That's the question that no conchie I ever knew could answer—'

'Stop your specious argument.' Miss Finlay cut him off. 'I said I had sympathy. I did not say I agree with them. But what I say to you is this: it appears that we do not need to wait for the Germans to arrive to kill our children. We have you to arrange that for us.'

'We are not enlisting children,' the sergeant said in a patronizing tone of voice. 'No children. The War Office has issued instructions. A lad must be eighteen years old before he can go overseas for active service. They can sign up when they are seventeen. But it's only after they turn eighteen that they may be posted abroad.' He turned to his adjutant. 'This is what happens when women get a smattering of education. They are unable to comprehend the whole situation.'

'I can understand what I read as well as any man.' Miss Finlay took a newspaper from her bag and smacked it down on the desk in front of the sergeant. 'It is reported here in the *London Times* that if a young man passes the army medical as being as fit as an eighteen-year-old, then he is deemed, *de facto*, to be eighteen years old and no one can complain. We know that you look for farm boys, because, due to outdoor life and hard physical work, they are taller and stronger than city lads.'

'A lad knows his own mind. Yes, he does. He can decide for himself when it's time for him to step up and be a man.'

'I declare that what you plan to do is illegal. Do not put pen to paper until I return.' Adjusting her hatpin so that her hat was more securely fixed to her head, Miss Finlay strode along the corridor to her office. A few moments later she came back with a pile of school registers. 'You will find in these registers lists of my pupils for the previous three years. Their ages are displayed beside each name. You may not enlist any name which appears there as those children will be of insufficient years to comply with army regulations.'

'You . . . I . . .' The sergeant's mouth fell open. 'You can't give me orders . . .'

Rob felt slightly sorry for him. Miss Finlay was very pretty and looked fragile. She smiled a lot, but when she was annoyed and got angry, she could be *very* scary.

'Sir, do not make any blustering protest to me.' Miss Finlay drew herself up to her full height. 'If you proceed to enlist any child in this village – any pupil from my school – I will report you to the Military Police.' She snatched up a pencil and slate and wrote on it. 'I have taken note of your name, rank and number, and I intend to write about this to the War Office, the Prime Minister, the King and – and Queen Alexandra herself.'

She swung round and stamped out of the hall. When she reappeared outside, there was a ragged cheer from the waiting women. They surrounded her to thank her and pat her on the shoulder.

Seconds later, Jed appeared. He was in a vile temper. 'You should keep your mouth shut, Millie Gowrie!' He aimed a kick at her.

Rob jumped in front of Millie to protect her.

'I was only trying to save you!' Millie began to cry.

Jed saw that his teacher had finished speaking to the village women and was looking over to see what the commotion was. He ran off, shouting over his shoulder, 'In future you mind your own business or I'll tell what I know about you!'

Miss Finlay gave Millie a handkerchief to dry her eyes. 'Millie, I think you are a very kind child – what you did was with the best of intentions. But Jed will not see it that way, so please stay away from him until he calms down.'

'He's always like that,' said Rob.

'No, Rob,' said Miss Finlay, 'Jed was not always like that. He was a pleasant and biddable boy until his father was killed in an accident. It was Jed who found his father lying under the stones that crushed his chest. Don't you remember him when he was younger?'

'Not really,' said Rob. All his life he'd played mainly with Kenneth.

'It has scarred his mind and he is permanently angry with himself and the rest of the world,' Miss Finlay went on. She looked at Millie. 'What is he threatening you with?'

'Erm . . .' Millie said awkwardly. 'I put a sandwich

in the bin one day 'cos I didn't like the filling.'

Miss Finlay raised her eyebrows. Half of her pupils were constantly hungry. They might swap a sandwich or a scone with one of their classmates in exchange for something else, but the idea that any child would throw food in the rubbish bin was silly. Millie was too young to understand that to be successful, a lie had to be believable. She was such an honest child – why then was she lying?

Rob noticed the expression on the face of his teacher. He too was uneasy. What secret did Jed know? Was it about the puppy? Nearly every time he'd been at Mill House he'd felt as if someone was watching them. Maybe it wasn't a ghost in the attic. Maybe Jed had seen them crossing the fields and followed them through the woods, over the wall and into the gardens of Mill House and discovered the hut with Sandy inside. If he had, Rob believed that Jed was mean enough to report them. Would the Army Procurement Officer come round to their cottage and fine them a massive amount of money?

It could be even worse than that. He'd warned them

against disobeying army orders, so he might put them on a charge and they would end up in prison. Was hiding the puppy serious enough to be considered treason? Rob shuddered. People found guilty of treason were executed.

CHAPTER NINETEEN

'Do you think Jed knows about Sandy?' Millie asked Rob the question as soon as they were alone. 'Do you think that's what he meant when he said he'd tell on me?'

'He can't know about Sandy. Jed just . . . blusters.' Rob used the word he'd heard his teacher say to the recruiting sergeant. 'It's nothing for us to worry about.' He was trying to reassure his sister, but he *was* worried. Jed went into the woods to snare rabbits as his mother barely scraped by on the small amount of money Jed's sister sent home. He must have seen them going to visit the puppy. Most likely it was he who'd moved the piece of wood across the door of the shed to find out what was inside.

'I think Jed is jealous of us 'cos he doesn't have a daddy at all,' said Millie.

Rob had a glimmer of understanding as he recalled his teacher saying Jed had been the one to find his father's body. 'Maybe Miss Finlay is right, then,' said Rob. 'Jed says nasty things to upset people because he's angry.'

'Should we move Sandy from the shed and put him someplace else?'

'Maybe we should,' said Rob. 'But meantime, let's get along home and see how Mummy is doing.'

'I think she's getting well again,' said Millie. 'She said she'd collect the eggs herself today.'

Their mother did seem in better spirits when they got home. In the past month she'd not bothered to organize their after-school chores or check they were done properly. Today, however, she was waiting with Nell at the door of their cottage, holding a brown paper bag. 'I want you to take these extra eggs to Jed's mother.'

'Take eggs to Jed's mother?' Rob asked in surprise.

'I've forgotten to do it recently, and her littlest one is quite sick. A runny egg is practically all he'll eat.'

'You've been giving some of our eggs to Jed's family?'

'We don't eat all the eggs our hens lay. Mind, don't say a word of this to any of the children who are at school – Pearl or Daisy, or that big soft lad, Jed.'

'Jed's not a big soft lad. He's always taunting me to try to get me to fight him.'

'He won't mean it.'

'It sounds to me as if he does,' said Rob.

'And he said he would kick me 'cos I reported him to Miss Finlay for trying to sign up for the army,' Millie joined in.

'You shouldn't let other people's behaviour affect your own – especially when performing acts of kindness. Go now, while Jed is working at Glebe Farm, and he won't see you do it. Leave them quietly on their doorstep.'

'But why should we give them our eggs?' Rob demanded.

'It's a neighbourly thing to do.' Rob's mother handed him the bag. 'And I'm returning a favour, family to family.'

'What favour has Jed's family ever done us?'

'Who do you think did our washing when I took to my bed, so ill in spirit that I could not cope?'

'Jed's mother?' Rob was astounded. 'She's too busy with her wee bairns to look after us.'

'Yet she did it,' his mother said. 'She's been coming along here with her sick baby happed up in a blanket on her shoulder and the wee one trailing at her skirts. She'd boil up the water, get the washboard out, scrub the clothes and then go on her way again.'

By the time Rob had run the errand for his mother and done the rest of his work, it was supper time. Afterwards, exhausted with the extra effort of her day, his mother went to her room to rest. Nell lay down in front of her bedroom door. Rob decided to leave his dog there. He'd no intention of staying any length of time with Sandy that evening. It was getting dark as he and Millie set out for the woods with the pup's food and fresh water.

'I've had a thought,' said Rob as they hurried along.

'You have the best ideas,' Millie said loyally.

'Well, if Mill House is going to be off limits, then perhaps we *shouldn't* move the puppy away from there. Perhaps the shed in the bushes is the safest place for Sandy.'

'But how will we look after him?'

'We'll not cross the lawn, but go the long way round, keeping to the bushes and trees that grow along the wall. And we can cut branches of evergreen and cover the roof of the hut so that no one will notice it if they look out from the rooms in the new clinic. I'll find Dad's telescope and make our own fire step to set it on so that we can have a lookout post like they do in the trenches. We'll be able to see anyone approaching.'

'Like bears and wolves?'

'There's no bears in Britain any more,' said Rob.

'Well, wolves, then.'

Rob thought maybe there were one or two in the remote forests of the Highlands. 'There are no wolves so far south,' he said. He didn't want to say to Millie that it wasn't bears and wolves he was concerned about.

There was no time to exercise the puppy. They hurriedly changed the straw and the water and left. Shadows were all around as they made their way through the bushes, across the lawn, to the top of the wall.

Millie climbed down the other side and caught the haversack. Before swinging himself over, Rob took one last glance back at the house.

His heart lurched in his chest.

In the end attic window, quite clearly visible, stood a figure in white. It was pressing its face against the glass, staring out into the night with huge empty eye-sockets.

CHAPTER TWENTY

'What is it?'

'Nothing,' Rob answered Millie, his breath coming in short ragged gasps. 'Nothing at all.'

He scrambled down from the wall. In the gathering darkness the twisted shapes of the tree trunks loomed, menacing. A wind rose, whining in branches overhead. Rob cried out in alarm as a crow flapped up in front of them.

'What's wrong?' Millie asked.

Rob pulled her along by the hand. 'Don't be so slow.'

It was only when they were out of the woods that his heart stopped battering about. If Jed was following them, then it would be like him to try to scare them. Rob was angry at himself for getting in a state. Ghosts didn't exist.

'Look!' said Millie. 'There's Jed.'

I was right, Rob thought. Jed was always thinking up rotten tricks to play on people. He glanced behind, but Millie was pointing towards Glebe Farm, where Jed was slouching across the fields. He must be on his way home, having finished his after-school work. There was no way he could have been the ghost in the house and then got ahead of them and be coming from the farm.

Rob decided he wouldn't tell Millie what he'd seen. He wouldn't tell anyone, not even Kenneth. His friend would laugh at him or want to go in a gang and search the old house – then it might come out that he was hiding a puppy. It was best that his classmates did as Miss Finlay advised and stayed away from Mill House.

Therefore it was totally unexpected when, the next day, posters were put up in the village inviting everyone to the grand opening of the clinic.

'How marvellous!' said Miss Finlay. 'I'm so glad they've

decided to do that, rather than being secretive about the fact that shell shock exists. The public should be aware that people who have suffered nervous debility can be rehabilitated.'

'Mrs Shelby is really happy,' Millie told Rob. 'Wagons delivering all sorts of things are driving through Glendale and she's had new customers and lots and lots more gossip to tell us.'

During the two weeks that it took to refurbish Mill House Rob and Millie cut branches of evergreen to use as camouflage. Rob nailed netting on the roof and walls of the potting shed to hold it in place. Anyone looking out from the top windows of Mill House wouldn't notice it among the shrubbery.

On the opening day it was Mrs Shelby, in a grand hat with feathers floating above, who led a column of villagers up the driveway to what was now known as Mill House Clinic.

Rob asked Millie not to try to persuade their mother to come along. He left Nell with her in the cottage that afternoon. He needed to be on his own for what he planned to do.

As he'd anticipated, groups of visitors were given guided tours of the public rooms downstairs, the bedrooms on the first floor, and even the staff quarters on the second floor. But when they came to a staircase leading to the third floor – the attic rooms – there was a barrier across the landing:

STRICTLY PRIVATE – NO ENTRY

STAFF ONLY

Rob peered up the stairwell. It was from a window in a room on that floor that he'd seen the ghostly figure watching them. He whispered to Millie, 'You go downstairs with the rest of the group. I want to explore the attic floor. Try to talk a lot so they don't notice I've gone.'

His sister didn't need any encouragement. Talking was something that Millie was good at. Rob saw her aim straight for the doctor who was their guide and bombard him with questions.

He studied one of the medical charts pinned to the wall, and then, as the rest of the group made their way downstairs, slipped under the barrier and ran lightly up to the attic floor.

The corridor stretched ahead of him. Six doors – six rooms to investigate. Now that he was here, Rob wasn't sure what he was looking for. A ghost? Ghosts didn't exist. But there *was* something strange happening in the house.

Most of the doors were standing open. Rob tiptoed along, peeking inside. Five ordinary rooms, each with two windows looking onto the front lawns: a couple of offices, a room with a cot bed and wardrobe, a bathroom and a kitchen. He came to the sixth door. It was shut. Cautiously Rob put his ear to the panel. Silence. He tried the door handle. It was locked. Then, from the stairwell, he heard voices. People approaching!

Rob skipped into the bathroom.

Two men. Arguing.

'These people being in the clinic is holding up my work.'

The voice was familiar. Rob peered through the gap

behind the door to see who was speaking. It was the older man with the beard and glasses he'd seen when hiding in the bushes with Millie.

'It's only for one day, Professor Holt.' His companion was placating him. 'Showing the locals over the house satisfies their curiosity. It means they'll be less inclined to wander in to see what's going on. Prevents them from discovering who we really are.'

Professor Holt gave a grim laugh. 'You are right. Perhaps the villagers would not be so friendly if they knew what we are actually doing to the soldiers here.'

'Indeed. That is why we must establish good public relations from the beginning. Now I should go downstairs and smooth over any awkward moments. You remain out of sight, for it's possible that someone could pick up on your speech as having a German accent and start asking questions.'

German accent!

Rob reeled back. Could these men be German spies?

When the other man had gone, Rob saw Professor Holt

take a key from his waistcoat pocket. He unlocked the door of the room at the end of the corridor. Then he went inside and locked it behind him.

As Rob rejoined Millie in the garden, his brain was whirling – thoughts and suspicions tumbling over each other. What were these men doing to British soldiers in the clinic? Rob stared up at the front of the building. Thirteen windows stared back at him. It struck him that the last window, the thirteenth, was in the room at the end of the corridor. The room with the locked door.

The same window where he'd seen the ghost soldier.

CHAPTER TWENTY-ONE

But instead of staying away once the clinic was up and running, the villagers of Glendale did the opposite. A constant stream of visitors left gifts of soap and knitted goods, packets of tea and sweets. Offers of assistance poured in – to nurse or read to the wounded men.

Within a few days a notice went up in the post office announcing that the officer in charge of Mill House Clinic, Major Cummings, would hold a public meeting in the village.

Rob was standing beside Millie when the major marched into the school hall. His eyes widened as he heard him speak and realized that Major Cummings was the officer he'd overheard talking with Professor Holt in the attic corridor on the clinic open day. The man who had said: *Now I should go downstairs and smooth over any awkward moments.*

Rob concentrated his gaze on Major Cummings. He seemed perfectly normal as he chatted to Miss Finlay and Mrs Shelby. Thanking the villagers for their generosity, he asked that, instead of them making the trip to Mill House, a member of the clinic staff would call regularly at Glendale post office to collect any donations.

'Only relatives of the patients will be allowed to visit, and a special pass will be issued for this purpose.' Major Cummings indicated a table where an army officer sat with papers and cards in front of him. 'If you have been informed that you have a relative in Mill House Clinic, please speak to my adjutant, Doctor McKay, who is an experienced psychiatric doctor. If, in his opinion, the soldier is able to receive visitors, then he will give you a visiting pass. Every Sunday afternoon any patient who is fit enough to have a visitor will be in the main drawing room. Please understand that these regulations are necessary for the welfare of our soldiers.'

As the people around him murmured agreement, it occurred to Rob that these arrangements also made it easier for Major Cummings and Professor Holt to keep secret whatever they were doing.

Millie nudged him. 'We need to get a visiting pass so we can go and ask the soldiers questions to help us find Daddy.'

'Yes,' said Rob. He had another reason for obtaining a pass. He wanted to find out what was happening in the locked attic room of Mill House. 'But I don't see how we can get one.'

'Look!' Millie pointed to where Mrs Otterby was speaking to Dr McKay. 'Maybe Jack's in the clinic. We could go with her at visiting time.'

But when they approached Mrs Otterby, she was dabbing a tear from the corner of her eyes. 'We got a letter telling us that Jack is to be sent to Mill House Clinic,' she told them, 'but Doctor McKay says we've not to get a pass at the moment. He'll let us know when Jack's well enough to have visitors.' She patted Millie on the head. 'I'll send word to let you know when that happens. Then you can come along with me. Jack would like that, I'm sure.'

Millie's shoulders slumped. 'We're never going to get any news about Daddy.'

Rob heard the quaver in his sister's voice. Over the last weeks two more hospital trains had gone up the line, and both times Nurse Evans had stood at the door of a carriage shaking her head.

'It could be months before we can visit the clinic.'

'Maybe not,' said Rob as a thought entered his head. 'If Jack Otterby has been sent to Mill House, then there's a chance that . . .'

'What?' asked Millie.

But Rob had left her and was standing in front of Dr McKay. 'Sir,' he said in his most polite voice, 'I'd like to enquire if a soldier we know is to be treated in Mill House Clinic. He is very close to our family,' he added.

'Name?'

'Private Ames.'

'Regiment?'

Rob froze. He tried to visualize the scene inside the last carriage of the hospital train. The soldier kneeling, eyes tight shut, mumbling to himself.

Dr McKay looked puzzled. 'Private Ames cannot be so close to your family if you do not even know the name of his regiment.'

'But he is!'

'When were you last in touch with him?'

'Not long ago. We know what's wrong with his eyes.'

'Spending time talking to people who suffer nervous debility does help.' Millie appeared beside Rob, quoting what Nurse Evans had said. 'People say I'm very good at talking and Private Ames likes my plum-jam sandwiches.'

'Indeed.' Dr McKay smiled. 'I don't wonder.'

In his mind's eye Rob saw Private Ames reaching to take a sandwich from Millie's basket . . . his regimental badge: a running horse.

'The West Yorkshires,' Rob said. 'Private Ames is with the West Yorkshire Regiment.'

'Are you a relative?'

'He's a cousin of my father's.' Rob realized he was becoming more adept at lying.

'It requires an adult to apply—' the doctor began.

'But our daddy is missing.' Millie gave a sob. 'Missing in action.'

Rob was finding it hard to tell whether his sister was really upset or turning tears on for effect. He decided he might as well pitch in too, so he put his arm round her shoulder. 'There, there,' he consoled her in what he hoped was a sympathetic manner.

'And Mummy has been so sad since the telegram arrived that she wasn't able to come out today.' Millie increased the volume of her sobs.

'Oh, I see.' Faced with a crying child and an utterly determined boy, Dr McKay asked for their surname. Then he wrote *Gowrie Family visiting Private Ames* on one of the official visiting passes. 'You'll be glad to know that your cousin is on the mend. He is allowed to have his hands free as he no longer scratches at his eyelids. You may visit him on Sundays, from two p.m. until four p.m.'

'Thank you, sir,' said Rob.

'I hope you have word about your father soon,' the doctor said as he gave Rob the pass.

The following Sunday afternoon, when Rob and Millie visited the clinic, was one of driving rain.

The nurse on duty read their visitor's pass. She looked beyond them to the front door. 'Don't you have a parent with you?'

'Our mother is unwell.' Rob's heart sank. It looked as if they wouldn't be admitted unless an adult was with them. But he'd reckoned without Millie.

'And Daddy is missing in the war,' Millie said. She sniffled and rubbed her eyes.

'Oh, I'm sorry to hear that.'

'I've brought Private Ames some sandwiches with jam that Mummy made.' Millie held up her basket. 'He does love jam sandwiches.'

'I think Private Ames is in the drawing room,' said the

nurse. 'You can take off your wellington boots while I go and check.'

Rob and Millie put their boots on the bottom of the hallstand. Photographs were ranged along the wall. One showed a young man in army uniform. Rob looked more closely. On it was written:

Edward – October 1914

October was the month their father had gone away.

'Is he the ghost soldier?' Millie raised herself onto her tiptoes to look at the photograph.

'There's no such thing as ghosts,' Rob said automatically. 'Look, the nurse is beckoning to us.'

There were half a dozen men in the drawing room. Some already had visitors sitting beside them chatting quietly. The nurse indicated a man who was sitting on the piano stool trying to pick notes out on the keys. His head was bent and he was mumbling to himself. Without hesitating Millie went over and touched him on the shoulder.

'Do you remember me? I'm Millie Gowrie.' She lowered her voice. 'I was on the hospital train a few weeks ago when you were in the end carriage with Jack Otterby. But I've not to tell that we were on the train or what happened.'

Private Ames raised his head. His eyes were still shut tight. 'I do remember you!' he exclaimed. He reached out to find Millie's hand. 'The girl with the plum-jam sandwiches. I don't suppose you've got any with you today?' he asked.

'I do!' said Millie. 'I always bring them with me when I'm going to see soldiers, in case—' She stopped.

'Did you think your daddy might be here?'

'He's not,' Millie said bravely, 'so you're welcome to have them, Mr—' She stopped. 'I don't even know your first name.'

'My first name?' Private Ames heaved a sigh that seemed to come from his boots. 'I think I am Humpty Dumpty.'

'Humpty Dumpty!' Millie laughed. 'That's not your name.'

'Well, if we've got Jack the Lad, and you're Little

Bo-Peep looking for a lost daddy sheep, then I can be Humpty Dumpty.'

'Why would you be Humpty Dumpty?' Millie asked him.

'Because I'm broken in bits.'

'Not every bit of you is broken,' she said. 'Just a little bit of you is broken. And the doctors and nurses will try to mend you.'

'All the King's horses and all the King's men couldn't put Humpty Dumpty together again.'

'You're *not* Humpty Dumpty,' Millie said firmly, 'and Doctor McKay is a nice doctor. It might take a long while, but he will help you.'

'Will you come and visit me?'

'Of course I will,' said Millie. She glanced at Rob. 'We could visit any of the sick soldiers.'

'Not all of them,' Private Ames said. 'You can't visit all of them – only the ones who can come downstairs on a Sunday afternoon. That is, only the ones they allow to come downstairs.'

'Is anyone from the Border Guards regiment in the clinic?' Rob asked.

'Shhh!' Private Ames put his finger to his lips. 'Don't be getting me into bother. We've not to say who is here and who isn't.'

'We know that the soldier who was in the train with you is here,' said Rob. 'Jack Otterby. How is he doing?'

'Jack the Lad? He's Jack o' Lantern now. Sleeps when it's light and gets up when it's dark. Wanders in the gardens with his lamp, looking for German spies. Says there's one right here in this clinic.'

Rob's breath caught in his throat. 'Who does he think is a German spy? Is it one of the doctors?'

Private Ames put his hand to his brow. 'The German spy is inside Jack's head. Even I am not crazy enough to believe him. The magic beans don't work for him. That's what they keep giving us. Magic beans to make us better. But some are too sick. Like me. Poor old Humpty Dumpty will never be the way he was before,' he said sadly. A long tear oozed from under his eyelid.

Millie put up her finger to catch it. 'You can make a wish,' she said, 'if you catch your own tear and taste it.' She held it to his lips.

The soldier put out his tongue. 'It's salty,' he said.

'That's because it's magic,' Millie told him. 'Did you make your wish?'

'I'll do it now. Do you want to know what I wished for?'

'No. You must keep it a secret – otherwise it will not come true.'

'If it does come true,' Private Ames said, 'you'll be the first to know.'

'That will be why Jack can't have visitors, if he only gets up when it's dark,' Rob said to Millie as they left Mill House at the end of visiting time.

'But Nurse Evans said that stressed soldiers need to talk to someone.'

'Jack didn't talk to us,' said Rob. 'Well, not in a way that made any sense.'

'He talked to Nell.'

'Oh!' said Rob. 'So he did.' Millie was right. Jack had been much more relaxed speaking to Nell.

'You're thinking of a plan.' Millie was watching Rob's face. 'I can tell.'

'I could come back at night with Nell,' said Rob, 'when Jack is outside in the gardens, and see if he can tell me what happened to the Border Guards.'

'I'm coming with you,' said Millie.

'No you're not,' said Rob. 'It's too dangerous.'

'There's no danger that Nell can't protect us from.' Millie gave Rob a hard stare. 'Unless you've only been pretending that you don't believe in ghosts.'

Rob looked away. His sister must have picked up on his change of mood the night he'd seen the white figure at the upstairs window of the big house.

Sensing his discomfort, she went on, 'If you go without me, I'll follow you and that would be worse 'cos I'd be walking across the fields and through the woods on my own. You can't stop me 'cos you can't report me to any adult.' Millie stepped in front of him to block his way and folded her arms. 'Well?' she demanded.

Rob flung his hands in the air. 'All right, then! We'll both come back here tonight after Mummy has gone to bed.'

CHAPTER TWENTY-TWO

Rob didn't like to admit it, even to himself, but he was actually glad of Millie's company that night when they returned to the big house.

The moon was bright in the sky, but Rob kept the shutter of the storm lantern open as they entered the wood. He wanted light around them to scare away any nocturnal creatures scuttling in the undergrowth.

Private Ames had told them that he and Jack shared a room and he knew that Jack sneaked out through the coal cellar. When Ames had asked Jack what he was doing, Jack had said not to worry, that he'd patrol round the house all night, staring up at the windows and keeping guard for him.

Millie had brought her basket of sandwiches and Rob a blanket, which he draped around their shoulders as they sat under a willow tree and waited.

It was Nell who alerted them by standing up, her nose pointing towards the house.

Rob tapped Millie on the shoulder. Within the dark entrance to the coal cellar was a denser shade. The outline of a man, moving slowly. Without warning he dashed across the grass to the shelter of the bushes. It was Jack. He was dressed in his army uniform and, holding a stick in his hands, pacing up and down.

'What should we do?' Millie whispered.

'We can't call out his name or approach him,' said Rob, 'in case he raises the alarm.'

'Send Nell,' she suggested.

Rob knelt and spoke to his dog. Nell padded across the lawn. They saw Jack bend down and heard him speak her name in recognition. Then he peered into the darkness. 'Who goes there?' he demanded. 'Friend or foe?'

'Friends,' said Millie. 'It's Millie and Rob come to visit you, Jack.'

'Advance and be recognized,' he commanded.

Without hesitation Millie ran silently to meet him. Rob followed her, arriving in time to hear her ask, 'What are you doing, Jack?'

Jack peered suspiciously at her, then Rob. Nell nudged his leg and his body relaxed. 'I'm patrolling the perimeter,' he told them. 'It's up to me. No one else sees the danger. I've got to keep a lookout for German spies. If I catch any, then I know how to deal with them. See! I stole this yesterday!' Moonlight gleamed white on the steel object he was holding up.

Too late Rob realized what he'd thought was a stick in Jack's hand was a bayonet. He backed off, trying to pull Millie with him. But she was too nimble. Sidestepping quickly, she held out the basket of sandwiches to Jack, saying, 'You could eat these sandwiches while I hold your sword for you.'

Jack hesitated for a second and then exchanged the

bayonet for the basket. He sat on the ground and, opening the sandwich parcel, stuffed the bread into his mouth.

Rob stretched out his hand to take the bayonet from Millie. Jack looked up, his eyes narrowing. Millie shook her head slightly. Keeping hold of the bayonet, she sat down beside Jack. 'I hope you like these ones. The plum jam is almost finished, so I had to use crab-apple jelly. I don't like it so much. But Rob took me berrying, and I've got brambles and raspberries ready to cook up.'

'There's not a lot of time,' Jack said. His face was twitching and his eyes slid this way and that. 'I need to keep watch.'

'I'll keep watch as you eat,' said Rob. 'Although you are in Britain now, you know.'

'I know that!' Jack spoke angrily. 'I'm not stupid. Or crazy,' he added. 'I've seen the enemy close by.'

Millie looked around. Within the house a few night-lights were burning, but everything was quiet. From the woods came the occasional hoot of a hunting owl. Apart from that the world was silent and peaceful.

'Where, Jack?' Millie asked. 'Where have you seen the enemy?'

Rob felt his stomach curl up in anxiety, terrified that Millie's question might set Jack off into some kind of fit. Yet he too desperately wanted any information Jack could give them.

Jack jabbed his finger towards the house. 'In there,' he said. 'Germans are hiding in the clinic. I've heard them plotting what they're going to do. They come out at night to kill us. That's why I've got this.' He snatched the bayonet from Millie. Then he pressed his face right up against hers, his eyes wild and staring. 'I've seen the ghost of a dead soldier.'

'The ghost soldier!' Millie let out a squeal of fright.

'Maybe it's not a ghost . . .' said Rob. 'Moonlight makes objects look eerie.' He recalled being out with his father one night when a silver fox streaked past them. They'd seen it disappear under a hedgerow. Out of the moonlight, its coat became red.

'Mill House is haunted,' said Jack. 'Everyone from these

parts knows about the ghost of the dead soldier who couldn't save his friend.'

'Have you told anyone else?' asked Rob.

'Not any more!' Jack shook his head. 'I mentioned it once and they gave me more medication and I slept for three days and nights. But when I'm hiding in the servants' staircase at night, I hear a man with a German accent giving orders.'

Rob started. A man with a German accent! It must be Professor Holt whom Jack had overheard, as *he* had done.

'What orders?'

'Can't rightly hear. Just snatches like, "I must have this," or "You must bring me that." The way he speaks, you can tell he's in charge.'

'Have you met this man?'

'No, but I saw the ghost soldier! I did. I saw him!'

Rob pulled Millie aside as Jack leaped to his feet. 'You don't believe me! But I've seen him. I tell you, I've seen him! You come here tomorrow night. Come late, after midnight, and I'll show you the ghost soldier!' He grabbed another sandwich. Then he ran back to the coal cellar and disappeared inside.

He was barely gone when Nell shifted her head, looking towards the end of the drive. Rob picked up Millie's basket and their blanket, and led her deeper into the shrubbery. A minute later a horse pulling a cart came trotting up the driveway. It was a long cart, with a lantern at the front to illuminate the road.

What type of goods were delivered to the clinic in the middle of the night?

As Rob watched, the cart swung across the front, heading towards the far side of the house. He grasped Millie's wrist and hurried round. The side door was open with light spilling out. Staying among the bushes, Rob and Millie crept closer. Professor Holt and Major Cummings stood there. Rob put his hand on Nell's head to keep her quiet.

The cart driver reined the horse to a standstill, got down and opened the tailgate. 'Got one here for you.'

'Be careful, man!' Major Cummings said sharply as the driver slid out a long wooden board.

'Why?' he asked. 'This lad's beyond feeling anything.'

Between them, the major and Professor Holt lifted the board to carry it into the house.

'It's a dead soldier,' Millie whimpered.

Rob could see the soldier's face quite plainly. He was a boy of about eighteen, his face pale as chalk, his jaw slack in the moment of death.

The clinic door closed. The driver clambered back onto his seat and shook the reins to leave.

'Don't know why they bother,' he said aloud. 'That one's a goner. Dead as a doornail.'

CHAPTER TWENTY-THREE

'Robert Gowrie!'

Rob blinked his eyes open as his teacher called out his name.

'You're dozing when you should be writing. Are you sick?'

'No, miss.' Rob sat up straight in his chair.

'Millie's teacher, Mrs Proctor, says that Millie fell asleep twice this morning. What were you two doing yesterday evening that you cannot stay awake in class today?'

Rob avoided looking directly at his teacher. It had taken him ages to get a sobbing, shaking Millie to sleep last night. He'd had to answer a dozen and more questions as he sat on her bed comforting her, and even more on the way to school this morning. His sister had finally accepted that the soldier they'd seen being carried into the clinic had probably died of his wounds during the journey in the cart. But Rob could not think why he'd been put into the cart in the middle of the night to be transported to the clinic in the first place. Why was the whole operation shrouded in so much secrecy?

'Well?' Miss Finlay was waiting for an explanation.

Jed swivelled in his seat to stare at Rob.

'Erm, my mother wasn't well ... she couldn't sleep.' Rob knew it was a shabby thing to do – speaking about his mother like that – but it was the only excuse he could think of.

'Oh, I see.' Miss Finlay's face softened in sympathy. 'Tomorrow's Saturday. I could come round in the afternoon and see if I can be of any help ...'

'No!' Rob cried out. The last thing he wanted was his teacher coming to his house. Jed smirked as Rob muttered a reply. 'Thank you very much, but my mother would get more upset, and she has medicine, and she'll not forget tonight – and I can . . . that is, Millie and I will make sure she takes it.'

'Well, all right, then' – Miss Finlay smiled at him – 'but please let your mother know of my offer.'

'I will. Yes, I will do that.' Rob nodded his head several times.

As soon as their teacher was busy at her desk, Jed leaned over. 'You can put your mother in that clinic that you and your sister are always hanging around. They'll know what medicine to give her.'

'Shut up, you!' said Kenneth.

Rob gave his friend a grateful glance and went on with his work. But Jed's remarks lingered in his mind. How did Jed know about their visits to the clinic? When Jed was out of school he went to work at Glebe Farm. He didn't have any free time to spy on them. Rob looked out of the class-room window. In the distance, the farm buildings were silhouetted on the summit of the hill behind the village.

Of course! Glebe Farm was so high up that it surveyed

the whole valley. Jed, working in the yard, could see anyone going in and out of the woods. Rob's chest tightened with tension. Standing there, Jed would not only have a view of Mill House, he'd also be able to see the shed where the puppy was hidden! He must have noticed them going in there and Millie taking the puppy out for exercise as she did every afternoon.

Rob turned his head. Jed was still watching him.

At the end of the school day Jed trailed after Rob and Millie on their way home.

As they went past the last house in the village, he came closer and, putting on Miss Finlay's voice, called out, 'What were you two doing yesterday evening that you cannot stay awake in class today?'

'Walk faster,' Rob muttered to Millie.

But when they increased their pace, so too did Jed. '*I* know what you're doing. You stopped me when I tried to enlist. I'm going to tell about you, and then you'll get into trouble.'

'Don't listen to him, Millie,' said Rob.

Millie turned round and stuck out her tongue at Jed.

In answer Jed scrabbled under the hedgerow for a lump of earth and threw it at them.

A shower of dirt rained down. Millie stopped to shake it out of her hair. Taking advantage, Jed closed in. Now he had a stone in his hand. If he'd been on his own, Rob would have sprinted for the cottage, but he knew that Millie would never be able to keep up.

He gave his sister a quick push. 'We're almost at the bend in the road. I'll wait behind and hold him off while you run home.'

The stone struck Rob on his leg.

'I'm not leaving you,' said Millie.

'Bring Nell to help me,' Rob told her.

Millie shook her head. 'It'll take too long. Jed could hurt you badly before I get back.'

Rob put his fingers in his mouth and whistled. It might be too far for Nell to hear, but it was worth a try. They'd reached the part where the road curved and they couldn't be seen from the village. Rob turned round, fists up, ready for a fight. Jed came on, grinning.

'I can thump you anytime using only one hand,' he boasted.

'Not both of us, you can't.' Millie put up her own puny fists and stood beside Rob.

'Need a girl to rescue you?' Jed sneered.

'Go away, Millie,' Rob said. 'You'll only get hurt. Jed is such a coward that he wouldn't mind if he hit a wee girl.'

Jed hesitated.

'If you take another step, I'll scream,' said Millie. 'Nell will hear me and come running 'cos I can scream really big screams.'

Rob knew that this was true. She didn't do it so much now, but when Millie was younger and fell over in the playground, her screams had been spectacularly loud.

Jed was remembering this too. He hesitated. Then he glanced towards the village. Kenneth had appeared on the road.

'Millie!' cried Rob. 'Kenneth will help me. You race to the cottage and bring Nell.'

Jed retreated. He picked up a few stones and lobbed them at Rob before running away.

Rob waited for Kenneth to catch up with them. Kenneth's house was in the opposite direction, so he must have come this way for a special reason.

'Is there a hospital train due?' Millie asked as soon as Kenneth was within earshot.

'Tomorrow,' said Kenneth. 'They got word at the depot. Dad came in off his shift there and told me. I thought you'd like to know. Lots of carriages. Coming through at first light.'

'Thanks for telling us,' said Rob. 'I' – he looked at Millie – 'we'll be there.'

Kenneth gave him a friendly punch on the arm. 'Good luck,' he said.

CHAPTER TWENTY-FOUR

A round midnight Rob was woken by Nell snuffling at his face. When he got downstairs, Millie was already waiting with her basket of jam sandwiches.

Rob lifted the haversack he'd packed earlier with a spare lantern, matches and a blanket. Moving so fast across the pasture land and into the woods meant they had no time to wonder about spirits or let fear build inside them. But once they were in the woods it was very different. The falling leaves rustled like ghostly cloaked figures hurrying at their heels. Spiky outlines of already bare branches threw weird patterns ahead of them on the path. They got to the wall, tense and out of breath. Rob hefted Millie up and over, and then followed her, to find Jack waiting for them on the other side.

'I'm patrolling—'

'– the perimeter.' Rob finished the sentence for him. 'Well done, soldier,' he added, remembering that Millie had said she thought Jack liked being praised.

'We may have a long wait,' said Jack. 'There's lots of activity on the third floor.'

'I've brought sandwiches.' Millie held out her basket.

Jack took it from her but kept hold of his bayonet in his other hand.

'They're not all for you,' Millie explained to him. 'We're going to meet a hospital train and I want to keep some in case my daddy is on it.'

Jack paused in munching his bread. 'I was on a hospital train,' he said. 'They handcuffed me to a post. But I found a key to unlock them. I'm good at finding things.'

'You must be,' said Rob, noticing that Jack had tucked the bayonet firmly under his arm as he was eating. 'How did you manage to get hold of a bayonet inside the clinic?'

Jack tapped the side of his nose. 'There's all sorts of storerooms in the basement, and when I was sent on patrol into no-man's-land, I learned to move like a shadow in the night. So I've got me a hoard of useful stuff hidden away in the coal cellar for when I need it.'

'The hospital train is coming through at dawn,' Millie went on. 'Do you think the ghost will appear before then?'

'Ghosts walk in the dark,' Jack said as they settled themselves under the trees. He offered Nell some bread and she went and sat beside him.

After waiting for half an hour, Millie shivered and said, 'It's colder tonight.'

Rob too was cold and he could see that Jack was becoming restless. His tremors had started up and the muscles on his face were twitching. Something was needed to distract his attention and prevent his thoughts from sliding away to the place where his nightmares lived.

'I've an idea.' Rob spoke to Millie under his breath. 'We could go to the shed . . .'

To his relief, his sister smiled and agreed. 'You always

have good ideas, Rob! It would be warmer, and I think Jack would like to see the puppy.'

'Puppy?' Jack looked distressed. 'War is not where a puppy should be. Bad enough for messenger dogs, but not for a pup, no.'

'The puppy is safe.' Millie took Jack's hand. 'Come and I'll show you.'

When they got to the bushes and Jack realized that he would have to crawl on all fours to worm his way through, his whole body began to shake.

'Barbed wire,' he said. 'Can't get through the barbed wire. Never get through the wire. They said the wire would be gone, but it wasn't. Coils and coils of it. Alfie was left hanging on the wire, and Patrick, and Joe Priestly, and—'

'Nell's going through,' Millie interrupted him. 'Follow her and you'll be safe.'

Jack frowned as she went into the tunnel that Rob had created. She called for the dog to come after. Nell waited, looking from Jack to Rob until Rob nodded his head. As soon as Nell went in among the bushes, Jack bent down and followed her.

The puppy was overjoyed to see them. Millie lifted him up and put him in Jack's arms. 'His name is Sandy,' she said, ''cos he's got a sandy-coloured tip on his ear.'

Jack's manner changed at once. He dropped the bayonet on the ground and went to sit in a corner, crooning to the bundle on his lap.

Rob made Millie a bed on the floor and wrapped her in the blanket. 'I'll keep lookout,' he said. He changed the angle of the telescope to train it on the house and watched until the lights glowing from the top-floor windows finally went out.

An hour passed, maybe more. Gradually Millie's chatter subsided. Rob clicked his fingers at Nell and pointed to his sister. Nell went to lie beside her to keep her warm. Millie reached out to cuddle the dog and immediately fell asleep. Jack sat stroking the puppy, and soon Sandy too was sleeping. Rob shifted position. He took out his grandfather's pocket watch and looked at the time. Gone three o'clock.

He could feel his eyelids drooping. He yawned, forcing his lids open, and stared out into the night. The windows of the house were blank.

And then . . .

One moment there was nothing. The next moment—

In the end window stood a figure in white.

With thudding heart Rob pressed one eye to the eyepiece. A wisp of cloud drifted over the moon. His vision blurred. He adjusted the focus. Then the cloud shifted and the moon showed through again. The figure in white moved closer to the window; close enough to be recognized.

It was the soldier who'd been taken, lifeless, from the cart last night.

Rob was looking at the face of a dead man.

CHAPTER TWENTY-FIVE

R ob let out a cry and the telescope tumbled from its stand.

'Attack! Attack!' Jack sprang up, bayonet in hand.

'Be quiet!' Rob shushed him. 'We mustn't wake everyone.'

Jack was trembling all over. 'Did you see him? Did you see him? Did you see the ghost soldier?'

'I saw something,' said Rob. His own hands were shaking as he climbed onto his fire step and replaced the telescope. He focused it again on the end of the house. The window was empty.

'You did see him, didn't you?' Jack's tone was one of desperate pleading. '*Didn't* you?'

Rob looked into Jack Otterby's eyes and saw the depths of his fear that he was going completely mad. Rob realized that how he answered this question was extremely important. Blood was thrumming in Rob's brain, but of one thing above all he was absolutely certain. Although there was nothing there now, a moment ago there had been a figure in white standing in the end window of the third floor of the house.

'There was a soldier standing at the window,' he told Jack. 'I saw him. The moon was out and I saw him.'

Relief vibrated through Jack. 'It's true!' he sobbed. 'I'm not hallucinating. You saw the ghost soldier too!'

Rob nodded.

'We have to go and capture him.' Jack was impatient to be off. He dived towards the door.

'Stop!' Rob looked at Millie. He touched her shoulder. She was in a deep sleep. He couldn't rouse her to take her with him. He'd put her in danger once before; he wasn't going to do it again. But he couldn't let Jack go racing off on his own waving his bayonet in the air.

'We must make a sortie,' Jack said. 'When they least expect it.'

'Wait,' said Rob. 'I'll come with you.'

Nell had stirred herself and came to him. Rob put his hand on her head. Much as he'd love to have his dog by his side, he knew that he couldn't leave Millie unguarded. 'Stay!' he commanded her. 'Stay here. On guard.' She stationed herself between Millie and the door as Rob followed Jack out into the darkness.

Within minutes they were through the bushes and in the coal cellar. Jack had discovered a way to climb up and down the chute that took the coal to the laundry rooms in the basement of the house, and this was his method of going in and out of the clinic.

'These are the servants' stairs from the laundry room that go right up to the top floor,' he told Rob.

Rob nodded. His mother had told him that servants in big houses always used separate stairs to go to and from their rooms so that they didn't meet their employers on the main staircase.

'There are bolts on the doors on each landing but I unscrewed them so I can get to any floor.'

Rob followed Jack up the stairs to the top floor. They waited, listening, but the only sound was the sputtering wick of the single lamp burning on a table in the corridor.

'Most of these rooms are offices,' said Jack. He pointed along the corridor. 'Was the ghost soldier standing at the window of the room at the end?'

'Yes,' Rob whispered. He had been in every one of the rooms except the one at the end. 'I think it's kept locked.'

Jack winked. 'Major Cummings has a spare key in his office' – he groped in his pocket – 'but not any more.' With a flourish he produced it.

Rob grinned in return. Obviously nobody had paid attention to Captain Morrison's instruction that a note should be put on Jack's medical records saying that he was good at stealing things.

They glided silently to the end of the corridor. Jack eased the key into the lock. By gentle manoeuvring, it yielded with a faint click. Jack clasped the handle. Carefully,

carefully he turned it and inched the door open. Rob was poised to flee, expecting at any second to hear a roar of anger. But no sound came to disturb the silence. Now the door was open wide enough for them to enter.

They slipped inside.

CHAPTER TWENTY-SIX

There was no one there.

Rob leaned against the door. His legs were trembling.

'Where is the ghost soldier?' demanded Jack.

'If he really *is* a ghost, then he can appear and disappear when he chooses,' said Rob. His voice sounded unconvincing even to himself.

Jack advanced into the room, bayonet held out in front of him, just like the soldiers in the park had taught Jed to attack the straw dummies. There was an extended screen in the corner behind the door. Jack wrenched it aside to reveal a wheelchair and some boxes.

These were the same boxes Professor Holt had carried into Mill House on the first night Rob had seen him. They were empty. What specialist equipment had they contained?

Jack prowled through the room, examining the items stored on the open shelves and the counter below: bottles and jars and lengths of tubing. He tried the doors of the cupboards underneath, but these were locked. Jack stooped and peered through the keyholes.

'There are papers and notebooks inside,' he said. 'I'll find a key that fits these locks, and then we'll know what the German spy is up to.'

Rob went over to a neatly made hospital bed that stood between the two windows. He put his hand on the covers. They were cold to the touch. No one had lain there recently. He looked out of the window. The hut was invisible from here. His efforts to conceal it had paid off. Even with the light of dawn beginning in the eastern sky, it blended perfectly into the surrounding greenery.

Dawn! Rob remembered that the hospital train was due at first light. Also Millie was alone in the hut. Rob was confident in Nell's powers as a guard dog, but his sister might be frightened if she woke up to find herself alone.

'I must go back to the shed,' he told Jack.

Jack readily agreed to leave the room. 'Retreat is best at this stage,' he said. 'I'll find some keys and we'll return and occupy this enemy trench.'

Before they left, Rob glanced around one last time. He couldn't work out what use could be made of this specialized medical equipment.

And there was something else, something not quite right, nagging in his mind.

He and Millie were in their usual position by the water tank when the hospital train drew up an hour later.

This train hadn't as many carriages as the previous ones, and the nurse and the medical orderlies had time to get off to speak to them. 'I've still nothing to tell you, I'm afraid,' Nurse Evans said. Bert too shook his head, and even the normally grumpy Chesney looked sorry for them. 'With the weather worsening, there may be fewer trains coming up.' Her voice was so gentle it made Rob want to cry. He guessed that she was trying to tell him more than what her words actually said. She was saying that there would be fewer trains, and so less chance of finding his father.

Millie's eyes filled with tears. Brusquely she handed her sandwich parcel to the driver and set off in the direction of their cottage. Rob knew that this time she was not pretending to be upset. In his heart he was glad that there wouldn't be so many wounded soldiers, but he was as downcast as Millie to hear that there would be a reduction in the hospital trains.

In the afternoon Kenneth called round to see if there had been any news and to ask if he wanted to go fishing. Rob shook his head at both questions. He went inside the cottage and closed the door. He was beginning to appreciate how his mother felt. This is what happened when you came to the end of hope. He and Millie had missed a lot of sleep over the last two nights, so for much of the day they lay on their beds and read.

Rob couldn't settle. He didn't want to look at the war

magazines that Kenneth had lent him. None of his military history books interested him. His mind was snagging on a thought just out of his reach.

In the evening they visited Sandy. Jack had said that he would leave a message in the hut when he'd managed to steal a key that might fit the locked cupboards in room number six. There was no note for them, so Millie took the puppy for a walkabout while Rob looked through the telescope. Visibility was poor. It had been a day of heavy cloud and drenching rain. Rob hadn't told Millie about being in the locked room with Jack. His little sister had enough to cope with – and in any case, he was trying to make up his mind as to what to do next. The ghost soldier might or might not be real – Rob still wasn't sure – but what he was sure of was that there was something odd about the top floor of the clinic. He couldn't discuss it with his mother, for the same reason that he couldn't tell Millie. And he needed more information before he spoke to any other adult, such as Mr Gordon or Miss Finlay. Rob tried to think what advice his father might have given him. 'Sometimes you have to do things by yourself,' he had once told Rob. 'If a job needs done and no one else is available, then go ahead and do it.' Here was a job that needed done, and only *he* could do it. Rob straightened his shoulders as he came to his decision. Aided by Jack, he would go ahead and investigate what was happening. And he wouldn't stop until he'd found out the secret of Mill House.

Next day, at Sunday visiting, the rain continued, but Private Ames wanted to walk outside.

'They're going to fix the lawn for us to play croquet,' he told them. 'Would you help me so that I don't hit anyone with my mallet?'

Millie slipped her hand into his. He held it to his lips and kissed it. Then he turned his face to the sky, and tears mingled with the raindrops on his face. When they came back inside, Private Ames went directly upstairs to his room.

'It rains a lot in Flanders,' the duty nurse said by way of explanation. 'When it rains here, it causes memories to surface, some of which the men would rather forget. You go off home and I'll fetch Private Ames a strong cup of tea.'

While he waited for Millie to put on her boots, Rob wandered down the hallway examining the rest of the photographs. There was one dated 1896, showing the front of the house. A game of croquet was in progress. There was a lady in a large hat standing with a mallet in her hand. She was looking up at the front windows, one hand raised in greeting. There was no one at any of the windows. Who was she waving to? Rob peered closer. His shadow moved over the glass.

There!

For a second he saw it. In the end attic window . . . a shimmering figure in white.

Rob stepped back in shock.

'Would you like a jam sandwich?' Millie was speaking to one of the patients who was sitting on a bench in the hall, watching her put on her boots.

'Mud,' the man said. 'So much mud. Ain't never seen so much mud in all me life. An' me from a farm an' all. Don't know what to do with so much mud. Can't get rid of it no how.'

Millie smiled at him. 'We put our boots by the fire, and then when they dry we take the mud off with a stiff brush.'

But the soldier didn't appear to be listening. 'Caked in it, so we were. And 'twasn't mud ye could walk in. If ye fell in a crater hole, then there were no way out. Bogged you down. Drowning in mud, so we were. An' the horses too. Once I saw them trying to get a horse out. Four hours they tried. Brought up a harness and everything. But wasn't no use. Couldn't budge it. "Get me a gun," the officer says. Then one of the lads – a boy, he was – crouched beside the horse and put his arms around her neck. "Ah, Bessie," he says, "it's time for the long goodbye. You've been a good pal and seen us through thick and thin, and I wish I was going with you, so I do." An' he starts to blubber like a baby.

'They'd to haul him off. He'd a tight hold of her mane and they'd to prise his fingers loose and lead him away. And his head was down, his shoulders heaving. And the officer says, "Well, I'll not ask any man to do a deed I cannot do myself." And he steps up to the mark with the gun ready.

'Pitiful beast knew what the end of the story was as well.

Just lay there. Rolled her eyes back and waited for him to pull the trigger.'

'The officer shot one of the British horses?' Millie's eyes were popping out her head.

The man rambled on. 'D'ye know there's even an army instruction how to do it. Best way o' killin' a horse. In the manual, so it is.' He put an imaginary gun to his temple. 'Bang!' he said.

'I don't think I like that story,' said Millie. 'Have you got another one you'd like to tell me?'

'The poor horses. They were our friends, no doubt about it. Pulling the guns and the carts and the food and the ammunition. But we weren't theirs. Oh no. Falling in their traces from overwork. And so one day I decided I'd had enough. We'd got caught by a clump of land mines, and a few of the lads disappeared. Gone' – he snapped his fingers – 'like that. And the subaltern who was with us got badly hit. Feet blown off. And so I reckoned I'd just leg it out of there while I still had legs to do it. And I took off my hat and flung it down, and everythin' else too. Pack and gear and trench spade and sandbags. And then I threw down me rifle, and the subaltern, he says: "You're on a charge for that, soldier. I'll have to escort you to Military HQ at the earliest opportunity."

'And I laughs, 'cos the sub, he ain't got no legs left fit for walkin'. So I says, "You gonna march me to the barracks?"

'And he laughs too and says, "I guess you'll have to carry me."

'So I light him a fag and sit and chat to him a bit, an' we talk about how I'd have to lock myself up and then shoot myself too for gross misconduct, but then I ain't got no rifle to do it with 'cos I threw it away. And then, after a bit, I notice that I'm the only one who's doing the talkin', and I realize he's gone somewhere else – to the better place the chaplain talks about. So I close over his eyelids and hope he's seeing more pleasant things than I am.

'And I go back up the line to the captain, and I report what happened to us, and he says: "It's a war. Men die. Pull yourself together. Where's your rifle, soldier?"

'So I looks at him, and then I hears myself screaming

and I don't know what I'm saying and it's all a bit crazy.

'And this captain is definitely going to have me shot. But I think, *Well, that's OK, 'cos I don't want to be there no more. I want to go to wherever the subaltern went to.*

'So among the boys waiting to be executed for cowardice, I'm the only one who wants to get shot. But do they shoot me? Oh no. It's the bleedin' British Army, so they don't do things that makes sense. No siree. I'm the one they decide to keep alive.'

Rob signalled to Millie that it was time to leave.

'Isn't the British Army supposed to shoot only German soldiers?' Millie asked.

The soldier nodded. 'I thought that was the plan too.' Then he paused, as if thinking about this. 'But now I don't think that's such a good plan, either. I've seen German soldiers. Dead and alive. And it's a funny thing . . . When they're alive they look like Germans, but when they're dead . . .' He stopped speaking for a moment. 'Little girl, when the Germans are dead, they look the same as us.'

And the man put his hands over his face and began to weep.

Rob took Millie by the hand. 'Mummy's waiting for us at home.'

'I need to go,' Millie told the soldier, 'but I'll come and visit you.'

'You will?' He spread his fingers to look at her. 'That'll be a first, then. No one ever visits me – not twice, anyway. No one ever listens to what I say.'

'I don't know if you should visit that soldier again,' Rob told Millie as they walked home.

'Why not?'

'Because . . . because Mummy might not like it.' Rob knew that was a lame response, but he couldn't think of an appropriate answer.

'I think Mummy *would* like it,' said Millie. 'It's the sort of thing she'd do herself if she . . . if she was . . . the way she used to be.'

'I don't think it's a good idea,' Rob told her. 'That man says things that are odd.'

'I think he says things that are true,' Millie replied. 'Maybe that's why nobody visits him, why nobody wants to listen.'

Rob looked down at his little sister. Had she fully understood that it was their own men, British soldiers, who'd been waiting to be executed? Because they were scared, or maybe ill inside their heads? Weren't you allowed to be scared during a war? It didn't seem right somehow.

'He shouldn't speak like that, even if it *is* true.'

'Why do you say that, Rob? Why are we told to always tell the truth, while grown-ups decide that they can tell lies?'

Rob was silent.

'Maybe if someone listened to him, he'd get well again,' said Millie.

'This is different. We are in the middle of a war.'

'I know that,' said Millie. 'But maybe if everyone listened to that soldier, the war might stop.'

CHAPTER TWENTY-SEVEN

S everal days passed before Jack left them a note in the hidden hut to say that he had a key for the cupboards in the room at the end of the corridor.

I got a key. Cum on Saterday when its dark.

While Rob waited impatiently for the end of the week, thoughts chased themselves endlessly around his mind. The lady wearing the big hat in the photograph dated 1896 must be the mother of Edward, the young soldier in one of the other photographs hanging in the hall of Mill House. She was waving to someone inside the house. Maybe the person at the attic window – the small figure in white – was

Edward as a young child, watching his mother from his nursery window. That would make Edward around twenty-four years old when he'd gone off to the war in 1914. Rob decided he'd have a proper look at the photograph next time he was at Mill House. Any photograph he'd ever seen had blobs and spots on it. Perhaps he'd only imagined a figure at the window. There was also the night when, coming back from the hut with Millie, he'd seen that blur of white at the attic window. And then there was what he'd seen through his telescope . . . But stories about the ghost at Mill House were being told in the village long before he'd seen the face of the dead soldier. Rob's head ached as he tried to work out what was real and what wasn't.

And . . . there was that something else; something which floated just under the surface in his mind, slipping away when he tried to reach for it.

It wasn't until Saturday night, when he was in the shed looking at the house through the telescope, that it was suddenly startlingly clear what had been bothering him.

'It doesn't add up,' Rob said aloud.

'What doesn't add up?' Millie was kneeling on the floor playing with Sandy.

'I see it now!' Rob's voice rose in excitement. It was like the last piece of a jigsaw puzzle clicking into place. 'The windows aren't right!'

'What's wrong with the windows?' Millie came to join him.

'Look!' Rob moved to let his sister onto his fire step. 'There are six rooms on the top floor and they have two windows each. I know because I've been in every one of them. Six times two equals twelve. There should be twelve windows on the top floor of the house.'

Millie put her eye to the telescope. From right to left she counted the number of windows: 'One, two, three . . . eleven, twelve, thirteen. *Thirteen!*' she exclaimed. 'There are thirteen windows on the attic floor.'

'Exactly! When Jack and I were in the end room, I thought there was something odd about it, but I couldn't work out what it was. It only has two windows when it should have *three*. Inside the house there is no thirteenth window!'

'Private Jack Otterby, reporting for duty.' Jack had arrived.

'Rob thinks there's a secret room on the top floor of Mill House,' Millie told him.

'Secret room?' said Jack. 'I knew it! Spies are hiding in the clinic! Tonight we'll find out what they're doing!' He showed them the small key he held in his hand.

With Jack, it was best to take things slowly, so Millie gave him the puppy to hold while they waited for the main clinic lights to go out. He settled himself in a corner and tickled Sandy behind his ear. Then he looked up at Rob and Millie. 'My mother and father are coming to see me tomorrow.'

'Oh, Jack.' Millie's face beamed a huge smile. 'I'm so happy for you.'

Jack nodded his head. 'So am I,' he said.

Rob looked at Jack's face. The nervous twitches around his mouth and eyes were less noticeable now. If Mr and Mrs Otterby were being allowed to visit, then the doctors must think that he was getting better. Rob suspected that he came to the hut at night to see the puppy, and slept there for part of that time – all the more soundly because he felt safe there. And if he got proper rest, it would make him calmer when he was awake.

Rob was relieved when Millie agreed to his suggestion that she should stay in the shed with Nell while he and Jack went into the clinic. 'At school on Monday, I'm going to tell Miss Finlay what's been happening. I don't want to worry Mummy. But' – Rob paused – 'if I don't come back by daybreak, you have to go straight to Glebe Farm and tell Mr and Mrs Gordon that Jack and I went to investigate a hidden room in the attic of Mill House. They'll know what to do.'

Millie gave him a hug and then put her arms round Jack. He smiled. Rob's heart flipped over. Since they'd first met him on the hospital train, it was the only time he'd seen Jack Otterby smile.

'Look at the windows.'

Once Rob was inside the end attic room with Jack and

the door was locked behind them, he pointed to the windows. 'There are *two* windows in this room,' he said.

'Yes, yes?' Jack was more interested in opening up the locked cupboards.

'I have been in every room on this corridor, and there are two windows in each. Six rooms. Twelve windows. But when you're outside looking up at the house, you can see *thirteen* windows.'

'There's another room – a room with a secret door?' Jack asked. 'Where the spies are living?'

'It can't be big enough for spies to live there,' said Rob, 'but they are definitely hiding something.'

'This is the end of the corridor. There's nothing else.'

Rob paced around the room. 'There is a secret room,' he said stubbornly. 'There *must* be. It's the only explanation.'

'Whatever is in here might tell us what they're doing.' Jack fumbled with the key in the lock. 'There's a metal cabinet inside this cupboard.'

A surge of cold air filled the room.

'It's a cold-store unit.'

Rob was puzzled. Cold-store units were used to keep food fresh. Why was there one up here rather than in the kitchens? 'What's in it?'

'Bottles,' said Jack. 'Glass bottles.'

'What's in them?'

Jack took one out. He brought it over to the window and held it up so that the moonlight fell across it. He didn't need to answer Rob's question. It was obvious to both of them what was in the bottles.

Blood.

Jack tilted his head. 'There's someone in the corridor!'

Rob looked round in panic. But not only was Jack Otterby's hearing acute, he was also very quick on his feet. He replaced the bottle, locked the cupboard door, grabbed Rob's arm and dragged him behind the screen in the corner as the door opened.

Pulse rate rocketing, Rob crouched down beside Jack. Through a gap in the screen he could see Professor Holt enter the room. The professor closed the door and went straight to the windows. There he unfolded the window shutter on the left-hand side.

Behind it was a door in the wall.

Professor Holt opened it up and disappeared inside.

In a single movement, Jack was flat on the floor. Before Rob could stop him, he was slithering on his belly towards the window. Rob had no option but to follow him.

'Blood . . . we need more blood.'

The secret door was ajar. Professor Holt was talking. Jack inched closer; Rob got to his knees so that he could see through the crack.

There was a single bed near the window. A body lay on it, the face corpse-white. Professor Holt was inserting a needle connected to a thin tube into the man's arm.

In a crashing second of shock Rob realized that the professor intended to drain away the man's blood.

CHAPTER TWENTY-EIGHT

Rob clamped his fist over his mouth to stop himself crying out.

'Please, please,' the man on the bed moaned. 'Please . . .'

Rob's first impulse was to rush forward and snatch the tubing away from the professor. It was Jack who kept his head. Silently he indicated to Rob that they should retreat. As soft as prowling cats, they left the room and made their way back to the shed.

'There's a German spy in the clinic!' Jack declared triumphantly to Millie. 'We have proof.'

The single thought throbbing in Rob's brain was that he must take Millie to safety as soon as possible.

'We're leaving,' he told her. 'We'll stop at Glebe Farm. Mr and Mrs Gordon will know what to do.'

'No!' Jack waved his bayonet in the air. 'We need to take Nell with us and mount an attack on the clinic. Now! When they least expect it.'

Instead of returning Sandy to his cage, Millie offered Jack the puppy to hold. 'Jack, you mustn't attack anyone,' she told him, 'else you'll not be allowed visitors for a very long time.'

'You can come with us, Jack,' said Rob.

'He'll be in terrible trouble if he leaves the clinic.' Millie looked from Jack to Rob. 'What did you see that upset you so much? The ghost soldier is supposed to try to save people's lives.'

'It wasn't a ghost that we saw,' said Rob. 'We found the secret room, and inside . . . inside—' He broke off, not wanting to tell Millie what he had seen.

'We saw a German spy,' Jack said again. The puppy was licking his fingers and his voice was steadier. He took a deep breath. 'He was draining the blood from a British soldier.'

'But how do you know he was a German spy?'

'We heard him talking in a German accent,' said Rob.

Millie looked at her brother and then at Jack. 'I don't understand,' she said. 'If this man is German, why doesn't he just speak in German?'

'Because I am not German,' said a voice.

Professor Holt stood in the doorway.

Rob shoved Millie behind him. With one hand Jack clutched the pup to his chest, gripping his bayonet with the other. Nell sprang in front of them.

Professor Holt put his hands above his head. 'I carry no weapon,' he said. 'And I repeat: I am not German. I am a Belgian doctor who is trying to save the lives of British soldiers.'

Jack shook his head. 'You are a German spy!' he hissed. 'We found the bottles of blood that you take from our soldiers.'

As Jack spoke, Rob was thinking desperately of how to escape. If he gave the order, he knew his dog would pen Professor Holt in the hut while they left to get help. But it would be best if they tied him up and gagged him so that he couldn't move or shout out. Rob rummaged in his haversack and pulled out a piece of rope.

'I do not take blood from the soldiers,' the professor answered Jack. 'Quite the reverse. I have been experimenting with putting blood *into* some seriously wounded men. I have been researching this field of medicine for years. After the war broke out, your government asked me to continue my work here as unobtrusively as possible.'

'I don't believe you,' said Jack.

'I assure you I speak the truth. Major Cummings, who manages the clinic, knows of the work I am doing on the attic floor.'

'I know he does,' said Rob. 'At the clinic open day I heard him speaking to you. He said you had to remain hidden as he didn't want anyone to notice your German accent.'

'Oh!' Professor Holt raised his eyebrows. 'Oh, I see why the confusion has happened. You thought Major Cummings said this because I am German, but in fact,

Major Cummings wanted to prevent people hearing me in case they mistook my Belgian accent for a German trying to speak English. I knew that Jack suspected there was something happening on the top floor, but I had no idea that anyone else did. You were both so brave to attempt to investigate.' He looked at Rob and Millie in admiration.

'Rob is very brave and clever.' Millie nodded her head. 'I just followed him.'

'It is good to have a brother like that,' the professor answered her. 'And good also that all of you are so loyal to your country that you try to trap someone you think may be an enemy spy. I feel that you are entitled to some explanation. Although blood transfusion is known in many countries, the techniques involved in storing blood are not. I have been working on a method of preserving donated blood to be used days later.'

'That's why there were bottles of blood in the locked room!' said Jack.

'Yes. And the room was locked to protect that secret just in case there were alien informers snooping around.'

'How did you know that Jack was suspicious?' said Millie. 'How did you know to come to this shed?'

'I heard you leave the attic room and watched from the window to see where you went. We were aware that Jack went outside at night, no matter how Doctor McKay tried to sedate him.' Professor Holt smiled. 'Jack is very good at making things disappear, including his medication.'

'I take my pills,' said Jack, 'in the morning.'

'Jack was becoming much more relaxed,' the professor went on. 'Doctor McKay thought that it was benefiting him being outside at night; that he had made a den somewhere and felt safer there. But we didn't realize he had friends.' Professor Holt reached out and touched Sandy on the head. 'My youngest son had a puppy dog. I gave it to him on his seventh birthday.' He took a photograph from his pocket and held it out for them to look at. Two young boys stood beside a swing in the garden of a large house. 'My children,' he said. 'I lost them and my wife at the beginning of the war. I was in Vienna at a Medical Conference when Belgium was invaded. Since then I have never been able to get home.'

'Our daddy went away at the beginning of the war,' said Millie, 'and he's never been home, either.'

'I'm sure he thinks about you all the time. I know I think of my own children every day.'

'Mummy got a telegram which said "missing in action",' Millie told him, 'and she has been very sad. But Rob thought of a plan. We go to meet the hospital trains when they stop below Glebe Hill. I bring plum-jam sandwiches 'cos Rob thinks Daddy could be on one of the trains and plum jam is his favourite.'

'I see.' Professor Holt swept his hands across his eyes. 'That is a good plan, Rob. I hope it works out for you. 'I – I . . .' He struggled to speak. 'Let me tell you of *my* plan. I thought, *I will dedicate my life to something worthwhile.* Faced with the destruction of my homeland and surrounded by death, I wanted to improve the blood-transfusion process to try to save soldiers' lives.'

'Oh!' exclaimed Rob. 'That's why you said, "Blood . . . we need more blood."'

'Indeed we do. Early methods involved direct

transfusion – drawing blood from a healthy person and putting it immediately into a needy patient. This can lead to complications for both individuals, and is not ideal in a war situation. But now we can chill the blood and it will keep for a short time. This will greatly advance the work and reduce mortality among the wounded men.'

'You take blood from the patients in the clinic!' Jack said.

'Absolutely not,' the professor replied. 'The work of the clinic is completely separate. The men being treated there are very vulnerable mentally and it would be unethical to ask them to donate blood. In any case, we were trying to keep the transfusion experiments secret, for it will be a great asset in helping our wounded soldiers.' He made a wry grimace. 'Although, obviously, we have not been totally successful in our attempts to stay hidden.'

'What are you going to do with us?' It was Millie who asked the important question.

Professor Holt pondered and then said, 'I'd like you to swear that you will speak to no one about the work that I am doing. It is of tremendous value and should be kept private for as long as possible.'

'We do. We will,' Rob said at once.

'Also, bring your mother to the clinic tomorrow afternoon so that Major Cummings can speak with her. I'm sorry,' he added as he saw the expression on Millie's face, 'for I will hazard a guess that she does not know what you have been doing here. It will be most uncomfortable for you to have to tell her, but you must do it.'

Rob dropped the piece of rope he was holding into his haversack. 'We should go home,' he said to Millie.

'That would be best,' Professor Holt agreed. 'Jack, if you feel safer sleeping here, then please do so.'

Still holding Sandy and his bayonet, Jack flopped onto the blanket on the floor and closed his eyes.

As they were leaving the hut, Rob asked the professor, 'So, what we thought was the ghost of the dead man at the attic window was your soldier recovering?'

'What dead man did you see?'

'One night a wagon brought a soldier to the side door.

You and Major Cummings took him inside, even though the wagon driver said you were wasting your time. The very next night I saw him standing at the window. I thought I was seeing a ghost.'

'Transfusion is almost miraculous when it works. A man can be on his feet within hours.'

'And the one I saw at the attic window the night after you first came here,' said Rob. 'Did that man survive?'

'What night was that?'

'One night before work began to change Mill House into a clinic, I watched you and Major Cummings carry boxes into the building.'

'Ah yes, we wanted to lock away our equipment on the top floor before the clinic staff arrived.'

'When I came back the next night, I saw a soldier at the end attic window.'

'But we didn't return until ten days later.' Professor Holt gave Rob a puzzled look. 'There was no soldier in Mill House that night.'

CHAPTER TWENTY-NINE

The following morning Rob kept himself busy with chores as he worried how he might prepare his mother for the impending afternoon visit to Mill House Clinic. As it neared midday, these thoughts were driven from his head by the arrival of Mr and Mrs Gordon.

Rob stopped sweeping the yard when he saw their horse and cart coming along the cottage lane. He went to meet them while Millie pulled some grass for the horse to chew.

'We're going to visit our daughter,' said Mr Gordon, 'but I thought I'd call by and let you know that there's a hospital train due at noon. A couple of railway workers who were checking the water tank this morning told me. Said the line was quiet on account of it being Sunday, so they'd put on an extra one today.'

As Millie was making her sandwiches, their mother came out of her bedroom. She picked up the bread knife to cut slices from the loaf. 'I hear you've been walking over to Glebe Valley to see the hospital trains pass by.' She paused and spoke directly to Rob. 'You do appreciate that there's only a tiny chance that . . . that . . . anyone we know . . . might be on one of those trains?'

Rob nodded, and blinked away the sudden tears that formed in his eyes. He and his mother looked at Millie, who was packing the sandwiches in her basket. Unspoken between them was the thought that at some point they'd have to try to help her understand that it was very unlikely she would ever see her daddy again.

'Nevertheless' – she put her hands on Rob's shoulders – 'I think it's a worthwhile thing to do. Waving to the men must cheer them up enormously. It will let them see that they're not forgotten by the people at home.'

Rob wondered if now was the moment to tell his mother

about the situation at the clinic. He'd also have to explain why the puppy was still alive: his mother still gathered wild flowers to place on the pretend grave in their garden. She piled a log on the fire and then sat down in his father's chair. Nell crossed the room and leaned her head on his mother's lap. Rob decided that he'd allow them to sit in peace together for a bit. He'd wait until he and Millie returned before letting his mother know what he'd been doing during the last few weeks.

The day was cold as they set out across the fields. A long skein of geese flew over, heading south. Winter was taking hold of the land. Leaves were falling so fast that the bare branches of the stripped trees looked like the spokes of an umbrella poking into the sky. The path in the woods was exposed, so that when they came down the slope of Glebe Hill they could see someone walking there. The person was coming from the direction of Mill House, and their furtive manner made Rob stop and look more closely.

It was Jed – with something bundled up in his arms. As Rob watched, Jed opened his jacket and placed what he was carrying on the ground. Then he took the string attached to it and started to drag it along the path behind him.

Millie, following Rob's gaze, was the first to realize what it was. 'Sandy! He's got Sandy! Jed is stealing my puppy!'

Loud though Millie's scream was, Jed was too far away to hear her.

'He's going to take Sandy to the vet! And then my puppy will be sent to the war and I'll never see him again.'

'No he's not,' said Rob. 'I won't let him.' He was just about to tell Millie to go and fetch Nell when a piercing sound rent the air.

It was the whistle of a train. Rob's head whipped round. The engine driver never pulled the train whistle on his approach to Glebe Hill. He only used it after the water tender was filled, to let those passengers who'd dismounted to stretch their legs know that the train was ready to leave. What was different about today?

A train was thundering through the valley towards them. The distinctive markings on the carriages showed that it was a hospital train. Rob and Millie heard the brakes slam on. With a tremendous clashing and grinding of metal on metal the train screeched to a halt at the foot of the hill.

Rob screwed up his eyes. He squeezed Millie's arm so tightly, his nails dug into her arm.

'There! Look!'

Tied to the window of the rear carriage and flapping wildly in the wind was the bright red cape of a Queen Alexandra nurse.

CHAPTER THIRTY

It was the signal!

Rob had never run so fast in all his life. The door of the end carriage was open and Nurse Evans stood there. 'Where is your sister?' she called to him.

'She's coming,' Rob panted, grabbing the rail to swing himself aboard.

'I'm glad you've arrived before her.' Nurse Evans bent over so that her face was on a level with Rob's. 'I do believe we have found your father, Rob, but' – she held up her hand before he could speak – 'I must tell you that he is dying. I am sorry to be so brutal, but it's important that you are made aware of this fact immediately. You will know best how to inform your sister. It's important that you do not give her any false hope.'

Rob heard the sound of the words, but their real meaning wasn't going into his brain. 'Where's my father? Where *is* he?'

Nurse Evans led him inside the carriage. 'Bert and Chesney are with him. They've nursed him constantly to keep him alive until we got here.'

Rob looked at the shrivelled form of the man who lay on a stretcher on the floor. Bitter disappointment overwhelmed him. 'That's not my dad.'

'I think it is.' Nurse Evans turned as Millie came up the steps and took her by the hand. 'He's been drifting in and out of consciousness since we brought him aboard. When he was lucid, all he spoke of was his wife, his two children, Rob and Millie – and, of course, your dog, Nell.'

'But it can't be . . .' Rob whispered. 'Daddy was so tall and big and strong and . . . and . . .'

'Captain Morrison told me that your father had been lost behind the lines for very many months. He avoided capture and survived by eating raw beets and turnips, but it's taken a huge toll on his health.'

'I don't recognize him,' said Rob.

'I do,' said Millie. 'That soldier has got a mole over his left eyebrow, and so has Daddy.' She knelt down and patted her father on the forehead. 'There, there, Daddy,' she said. 'We're going to take you home now.'

Nurse Evans shook her head and beckoned for Rob to follow her outside. 'Rob, this is very hard for you, but please try to understand what I am saying. Captain Morrison moved heaven and earth to find your father. He contacted everyone he thought might be of assistance and spent his spare time going through casualty lists, and eventually found him in a hospital in Rienne. Your father had undergone surgery which was successful, but due to the colossal amount of blood he lost, the doctors there termed his condition as "not expected to live". Captain Morrison told them that their patient might as well die at home as in the ward, and used all his influence to get him on a cross-Channel transport and a train going north. Please, Rob, take this opportunity of seeing your father as an unexpected gift, and be content with that.'

'Can't you do anything to help him?'

'There's only a certain amount of blood that any one person can lose. It takes weeks for the human body to replace even a pint. Your father cannot survive with the amount he has lost. There is no hope, I'm afraid.'

'But there *is* a way of replacing blood!' Rob cried out. 'I know there is. You take it from one person and give it to the other.'

'I know doctors are working on a safe method of transferring blood from one person to another,' said Nurse Evans, 'but it isn't common practice yet.'

'They're still experimenting with it,' said Rob, 'but it does work. I saw a man who was almost dead and then—' He stopped, realizing he shouldn't say any more.

Nurse Evans stared at him. 'Where? Where have you seen this done? You have to tell me,' she went on as Rob hesitated, 'if you think there's a chance of saving your father.'

Rob pointed to the woods. 'There's a special clinic there,' he said. 'It's mainly for shell-shocked soldiers. Jack Otterby is there, and so is Private Ames. We go and visit them.'

'I'd heard they'd set up a psychiatric unit for enlisted men in this area,' said Nurse Evans, 'but I don't see what that's got to do with blood transfusion.'

'We're not supposed to tell anyone, but we found out that they're doing transfusion trials on the top floor of the clinic.'

'That's all very well, but it doesn't mean that this would work for your father.'

'You said that his operation was successful but the blood loss would kill him.'

'Yes, but—'

'What's the hold-up?' An army captain had come along the line. 'Children shouldn't be anywhere near this train.'

'I'm performing an act of charity, sir.' Nurse Evans stood her ground. 'Rob and Millie have been meeting every hospital train searching for their missing father. Captain Morrison managed to find him and arrange for him to be on this transport.' She moved closer and lowered her voice. 'The man is fading fast. I was allowing them to say goodbye.'

'This is highly irregular.' The captain looked at Rob. 'Right, young man, do as the nurse tells you and then be off. We need to get moving.'

'We'll take him to Mill House Clinic.' Desperation had inspired Rob. 'Millie will run and bring Farmer Gordon with his horse and cart and we'll take my father to the clinic in the woods.'

The captain snorted. 'That suggestion is quite ridiculous.'

'*Please.*' Rob was aware that tears were running down his cheeks but he didn't care. 'Let us do it. It's his only chance.'

'I'm in charge of this transport. The man is dying. He must remain on the train.'

'If he's going to die anyway,' Rob pleaded, 'what difference does it make to you?'

'They've got a point,' Nurse Evans said. 'Whatever way you look at it, you said it yourself – he's a dying man. The farmer who will help him lives yards away. I've met him. He's a steady sort of a chap.'

'It's impossible. There are rules and regulations. That's the way the army works.'

'Yes,' Nurse Evans said sarcastically, 'and we've seen exactly what those rules and regulations lead to, haven't we?' She spread her hands to take in the whole train.

'Yes, but . . .' The captain hesitated.

'We know the outcome here. We've seen it a thousand times before,' she went on. 'If he survives the next hour of this train journey, we'll deliver a dying man to Edinburgh. In his condition he won't even get to see a doctor.'

'There could be serious repercussions—'

'Have a heart, man!' To Rob's amazement, it was Chesney, appearing at the carriage door, who cut across the captain's speech. 'If he reaches the military hospital alive, he might die alone in a corridor. And if it happens before we arrive, then the problem and the paperwork are ours to deal with.'

Nurse Evans rolled her eyes when Chesney mentioned

paperwork, but she spoke up to support him. 'We know the amount of bother that entails. It will only serve to delay us attending to the other men who need our care. The alternative is that we let him off here and he dies with his family around him.'

The captain hesitated.

Nurse Evans saw him falter and pressed her advantage. 'So many lives have been lost in this dreadful war – let us not also lose our humanity.'

'*Please.*' Millie had jumped off the train and was hanging onto the officer's sleeve. '*Please,*' she begged. 'If Daddy is dying, then we want to go and get Mummy so she can say goodbye to him too.'

The officer looked at her, at Rob, at the medical orderlies and Nurse Evans. He took off his cap and threw it on the ground. 'Blast this war!' he shouted. 'I'm going to speak to the engine driver. As soon as that hose is disconnected from the water tender, we are leaving.' He bent to retrieve his cap. 'And let it be known that I never saw or heard anything that went on at the rear of the train at this stop.' He marched away without looking back.

Bert and Chesney carried the stretcher out of the train and laid it down beside the railway line.

Meanwhile Nurse Evans stuffed dressings and iodine into a pillowcase. She scribbled on a piece of paper. 'Give that to the doctors at the clinic. It might help them decide what they can do.'

She put her hand on Rob's shoulder. 'You do know – and you must explain to the rest of your family . . . that there is little hope.'

'Yes,' said Rob, for he did appreciate the gravity of his father's condition; but ringing in his head were Miss Finlay's words to him:

A little hope is all that's needed.

'Good luck! Good luck!' Nurse Evans waved as the engine roared and the carriages clacked away.

'I'll be faster than you,' Rob spoke to Millie. 'You stay with Daddy and I'll go to Glebe Farm and ask them to come with their horse and cart.' He made to run up the hill and then stopped short.

'Millie . . .' Rob turned to his sister. He spoke in a stunned shocked voice. 'I've just remembered. It's Sunday. When Mr and Mrs Gordon called in at our house this morning, they were going out to visit their daughter for the day like they do every Sunday. They've taken with them the only horse around here.'

When she heard what Rob said next, the colour drained from Millie's face.

'Without a cart and a horse we've got no way of getting Dad to Mill House Clinic.'

CHAPTER THIRTY-ONE

Millie opened her mouth to let out a howl of grief. Rob stepped forward and put his hands on each side of her face. 'You're always telling me what a big girl you are. This is your chance to prove it. Bite your lip and try not to cry. Can you do that for me?'

Millie clenched her teeth together and nodded.

'Good girl,' said Rob. 'Listen to me. I want you to run home and get Mummy so she can come and say goodbye to Daddy.'

'Can't we take Daddy to the clinic? Please?'

'We won't be able to carry the stretcher. Daddy's too heavy for us.'

'We could drag the stretcher.' Millie wiped her tears and sniffed. 'Between us, we could drag it along.'

'Look at him, Millie. Blood is soaking through his clothes. We'd only make him worse. It's best you go and get Mummy.' Rob sat down on the ground, his shoulders slumped in despair. 'We can't do it.'

'Yes we can,' said a voice.

Rob looked up. A figure appeared from behind a tree. It was Jed.

'Leave us alone,' said Rob. 'You're not wanted here.'

Jed walked over and took up a position at the head of the stretcher. 'I'm big enough and strong enough to take the heavy end by myself. The two of you can take the other one together.'

'Jed!' Millie ran and threw her arms around his waist.

Jed pushed her away, but not roughly. Rob was still sitting there, his mouth half open in surprise.

'Come on,' Jed told him. 'If you want to save your dad, we need to hurry up.'

With the greatest care they hoisted up the stretcher and

set off into the woods. Jed was able to bear most of the weight, and as they reached the avenue gates, Rob suggested that Millie run on to alert the doctors at the clinic.

'Then they'll be ready to take Daddy to their transfusion room,' he said.

They stopped to let Rob take hold of both handles at his end of the stretcher. He was out of breath, but he could see that Jed's brow was covered in sweat. Jed wasn't as strong as he made out.

'How was it that you happened to be there when the train stopped?' Rob asked him as they moved on.

'Just passing by,' Jed answered without turning his head. 'Lucky for you.'

'It wasn't luck,' said Rob. 'What were you—?' He broke off as he remembered that, from Glebe Hill, he and Millie had seen Jed walking through the woods with Sandy. In all the excitement of the train stopping, he'd forgotten about that. But he couldn't mention that they'd seen him stealing Millie's puppy; not while Jed was carrying the stretcher. And now they were almost at the clinic.

As they crossed the lawn, the main door opened and Millie ran out. Hurrying behind her were Major Cummings and two medical orderlies. Bringing up the rear was Professor Holt.

Even after the stretcher was taken from him, Rob's knees were shaking so much he could hardly walk up the few steps to the front door.

It was Millie who thought to thank Jed.

'Forget it,' he said gruffly. 'I'll go and fetch your mother for you.'

Rob followed the doctors into the clinic and up to a bedroom on the second floor. But his heart plummeted as he saw the expression on their faces. Professor Holt read Nurse Evans's note, made a brief examination and then bowed his head. 'We can do nothing for this man.'

Millie looked from him to Major Cummings. 'But Rob said you might be able to save my daddy. He said you had blood you could give him.'

The major drew Rob to one side. 'Are you aware that your father is dying?' he said.

'Yes, sir,' said Rob, 'but—'

'Your sister told me how he came to be with you. I cannot believe that the army medical staff allowed you to take him off the hospital train.'

'Because we persuaded them that this was the only chance he had of surviving.'

'I am less qualified than Professor Holt in these matters, but even I can see that this only chance is no chance at all.'

'But you transfuse people!' Rob cried. 'I saw the soldier who was as good as dead, and you brought him back to life.'

'You see far too much, young man,' Major Cummings said abruptly.

Millie began to cry, but silently, tears welling up in her eyes and coursing down her cheeks.

'I am not without sympathy,' the major said. 'We'll make your father as comfortable as possible before your mother arrives. Then you can all sit with him until he passes away.'

CHAPTER THIRTY-TWO

R ob was listening to Major Cummings but he was watching Professor Holt.

The professor re-read Nurse Evans's note and handed it to Dr McKay, who had entered the room.

'Blood,' Professor Holt murmured to the doctor. 'We need more blood.'

Those were the same words Rob had heard him mutter under his breath as he'd leaned over the soldier in the secret room! And Rob now understood their meaning. The professor was running short of bottles of blood. 'The reason you can't save my father is because you don't have blood, isn't it?' said Rob. 'You've none left. That's what you were talking about last night.'

Dr McKay used his stethoscope on Rob's father's chest. 'Pity,' he said. 'His heart is strong. He must have been a fit man to survive what he's been through.'

'He was!' said Rob. 'I mean, he *is*. My father is very, very strong. Day and night he was out on the hills in the worst weather to bring in the early lambs.'

Professor Holt looked seriously at Rob. 'We don't have the resources to do it. Believe me, I would very much like to try. But I used the last of our stored blood this morning for the patient upstairs.'

'But you can transfer blood from one person to another!' said Rob. 'You told me that was an early method of doing transfusions.'

'It's a dangerous procedure, and we've no time to check if the donor is suitable. Everyone's blood is not the same. It can be categorized into different groups. In the note she sent, Nurse Evans has stated that your father has the most common blood group, which in better circumstances would be helpful to know, for mixing one group with another can prove fatal. In any case, no one in this clinic can donate their blood. All the staff have given as much as we dare take from them. No' – he smiled sadly as Rob held out his arm – 'no, I will not take blood from a child. It could damage you permanently.'

'Will you take it from me, then?' said a voice.

'Mummy!' cried Millie. She ran to her mother as she came into the room.

'I am this man's wife and I wish to give him my blood.'

'Madam' – Professor Holt inclined his head towards Rob's mother – 'your body weight is insufficient. It would endanger your own life if I did so.'

'I want to do it,' she said.

'Think carefully,' the professor said gently. 'Your children could be left with no parents at all, instead of having at least one. You cannot take that risk.'

'*I* will take the risk.' Jack Otterby stood at the door. 'I am strong enough.'

'Alas, not from you, either.' Wearily, Professor Holt

passed his hand over his brow. 'One of the conditions of my working within this clinic was that no blood would come from any patient being treated here. The person who is in charge of the main function of the clinic will explain the reason to you.'

'There is a code of ethics,' Dr McKay told them. 'The psychiatric patients in this hospital are in my care, and I will not permit blood to be taken from any man who is suffering mental illness.'

'You think I can't decide things for myself?' said Jack. 'You think I am mad?'

Dr McKay crossed the room to stand in front of Jack. 'I do not think you are mad. I do think you have suffered deep trauma, are sleep-deprived and overstressed, and have bouts of paranoia. Therefore you may make a decision that is not in your own best interests.'

'I feel well enough now.'

'You are indeed very much better, but in all honesty, I doubt if you should make major decisions on your own at this time.'

'Who does decide things for me, then?' said Jack. 'Who would you allow to decide what I can do?'

'At the moment' – Dr McKay hesitated – 'your parents are the ones best placed to know that.'

There was silence. Then Millie spoke up. 'Jack's parents are due to visit him this afternoon.'

'So they are!' Jack beamed at Millie, and turned and ran out of the room.

Jack's parents were overjoyed to see and hear him behaving almost like his old self again. Both Professor Holt and Dr McKay spoke to them, but it was Jack himself who persuaded them to sign the form. He asked that Rob and Millie should be there when he told everyone the reasons why he wanted to donate his blood.

'I broke down completely during an important attack,' he confessed. 'That's why I was sent home. A shell exploded right beside me. I tore off my clothes and began screaming and shooting my rifle at the sky. My friends went forward to die without me fighting at their side. I'm so ashamed that

I didn't help them. Now I've a chance to save the life of a fellow soldier, and it makes me feel as though I'll be worth something again.'

Mr and Mrs Otterby looked at Dr McKay.

'That seems like a sensible reason to me,' he said.

'The ghost soldier would like what you are doing, Jack,' said Millie.

As his sister spoke, a strange quiver ran through Rob.

Mr Otterby signed the consent form for the blood transfusion and then put his arm round his son's shoulder. 'I am proud of thee, lad,' he said.

Before Rob's mother was given a similar form, Professor Holt spoke to her.

'You do understand that this procedure may not work? We don't have time to test Jack's blood, but I am hoping that it is of the same common group as your husband's. It may not be, so this transfusion might even hasten your husband's death.'

'But without it he will certainly die?' Rob's mother

asked. When the professor nodded, she picked up the pen, signed the form and handed it to him.

'I'd like to stay, please, sir,' Rob said as Major Cummings instructed them to follow him downstairs.

'It would calm my nerves,' Jack said quickly as the major opened his mouth to refuse this request.

Professor Holt looked at Rob kindly. 'For a short time only.'

'I'll leave as soon as you say I must,' Rob promised him.

In the secret room on the attic floor Dr McKay placed two beds side by side while the professor prepared his equipment.

'Your blood will pass through a filtration unit,' Professor Holt explained to Jack as he swabbed his skin with dis-infectant and inserted a needle into his arm. 'We use sodium citrate to stop the blood coagulating, although . . . normally there would be more preparation time.'

Rob saw that his father's body was so inert that he scarcely moved as a corresponding needle and tubes were connected to his arm.

Jack winked at Rob as his blood began to flow into the tube and on towards the transfuse-vac flask. 'This is good strong stock going from one shepherd to another.'

Rob realized that Jack was trying to help him hold himself together and thought how their positions were now reversed. He smiled at Jack, biting hard on his bottom lip as he did so to stop it from trembling.

Within minutes the pallor of his father's face altered – from a wax-like grey to dirty white.

Rob squeezed his eyes closed and then opened them wide. Was he imagining this? No! Definitely – he could see the change – the texture of his skin was improving. But . . . there was a worry line along Professor Holt's forehead. And his father's breathing was less rhythmic. He was struggling for air. The sigh and stutter of each desperate intake of breath sounded loud in the quietness of the room.

'What's happening?' Rob whispered.

Dr McKay looked at Professor Holt. The professor gave a tiny shake of his head. 'We should disconnect.'

'I don't want you to stop.' There was a new confidence in Jack's voice as he spoke.

'Adrenalin?' suggested Dr McKay.

'It's not been used extensively. I've not had a chance to gauge its effects in cases like this . . .' The professor hesitated. 'I suppose . . .' His voice tailed off. 'Yes, all right.' He took a syringe from the sterilization unit, then glanced at Rob.

'Rob,' said Dr McKay, 'your mother and sister need support. You should go to be with them.'

Jack raised his free hand to his forehead. Rob felt his throat tighten, but he managed to nod and return the salute before he left the room.

Waiting was the hardest thing Rob had ever done. Downstairs, Mr and Mrs Otterby sat in the drawing room talking to his mother while Millie chatted to Private Ames.

'He's Jack the Giant Killer now,' Private Ames was telling her, 'ready to slay demons. I'm not surprised he volunteered to help another soldier. He was the same in the trenches. Always was a brave one, that lad.'

'You should tell his mummy and daddy that Jack is brave,' said Millie. 'They might think he shakes sometimes because he's a coward.'

'I will,' said Private Ames. 'And I'll tell you something else. A minute ago I thought I saw the sky – the blue, blue sky. But I know that I'm inside the clinic, so it cannot be true.'

'No, it cannot,' Millie agreed, 'for there is no blue sky today.' She looked out of the window. 'There are only grey clouds above us.'

'I love blue. My mother's eyes are blue.'

'Mine too,' said Millie. 'That's why my mummy bought blue material to make me this dress. She said it would bring out the colour of my eyes.' She frowned, then stepped in front of Private Ames. 'Can you see the colour blue again?'

'A little bit,' he answered her.

'And now?' she asked, stepping away from him as she did so.

He shook his head. 'It comes, and it goes. I don't know why.'

Millie tilted her head to look up at him. His eyelids were raised by the tiniest amount, letting in a thin sliver of light. She sat down on the rug and spread her skirt around her. 'Look at the floor,' she said, 'and tell me the colour you can see.'

'Blue,' said Private Ames. 'I see the blue sky.'

'Not the sky,' Millie corrected him. 'I think you are seeing my blue dress.'

'Glory be!' said Private Ames. He fell onto his knees and raised his hands to the ceiling. 'Glory be to the great Creator! I can see again. I have lived in darkness, but now I can see!'

Hours passed and the sun was setting when Rob left his mother, with Millie cuddled in her arms as if she were a baby, and took Nell outside for some exercise. He looked at the top floor of Mill House. The thirteenth window was empty.

Private Ames joined him, and together they walked up and down the lawn, driveway and garden paths, over and over, until a shower of rain drove them to shelter inside the clinic.

Professor Holt came to meet them. 'I will thank Mr and Mrs Otterby and let them know that their son has not suffered any ill effects through the giving of his blood. It's too early to say for sure,' he said, before Rob could open his mouth, 'but you might want to be the one to tell your mother and sister that your father's condition has improved very slightly. He is conscious and you may go and talk to him.'

Rob went into the drawing room. His mother and sister were asleep on one of the couches. Very, very gently he brushed his fingers on Millie's cheek to wake her up.

'Daddy is awake,' he whispered. 'Daddy is awake and wants to see you.'

'One minute only.'

Major Cummings stood at the foot of their father's bed

as Rob and his sister and his mother tiptoed into the room.

'Welcome home, Daddy.' Millie kissed her father's hand, which lay still on the bedcovers. He moved his fingers, but did not open his eyes.

'He is extremely ill, but he can hear you,' said the major.

Rob's mother's face was soaked with tears. 'Dearest William,' she said, 'you've come back to us at last.' With the gentlest of touches she stroked his hand. Then she stepped aside so that Rob could do the same.

Rob thought his heart would burst – his dad was here in front of him after months and months of absence! He gave his father the best handshake he could manage . . . and felt an answering response.

CHAPTER THIRTY-THREE

'Sandy helped too, didn't you, boy?' said Millie.

They were in Dr McKay's office a few days later, when he was filling out forms to update their father's medical records: his condition had changed from 'not expected to live' to 'patient making progress'. The doctor reached across his desk to pat the pup that Millie was holding.

'I agree,' he said. 'And if the two of you look after him, then I don't see any harm in him remaining at the clinic. It might do the men some good – Jack Otterby especially.'

'He's a stray,' said Millie. 'We found him in the woods.'

'Looks like a pure collie,' said Dr McKay, 'apart from the sandy bit across his ears.'

'That's why I named him Sandy,' Millie blurted out. 'He doesn't look so much like Nell as her other pups did— Oh!' She put her hand to her mouth as she realized her blunder.

The doctor smiled. 'Why do I think that I am missing something here?'

'The army requisitioned Nell's puppies to make them into messenger dogs.' Rob decided it was time to tell the truth. 'They came to take them away, and . . .'

'Ah . . .' Dr McKay nodded in understanding. 'And this fine fellow, being smallish and smart, somehow got overlooked.'

'Sandy wasn't really overlooked,' said Millie. 'Rob thought of a plan to hide—' She stopped before Rob could kick her ankle.

'It would be a great loss to the clinic if he were removed,' said Dr McKay. 'Sandy's contribution to patient morale is of paramount value. I'd say he helped Jack Otterby's recovery along by several months.' He picked up his pen and wrote on some headed notepaper. 'There you are. I'm issuing an official certificate that makes Sandy an essential member of the staff of Mill House Clinic. He is now in a reserved occupation and cannot be requisitioned by the armed forces.'

'I wondered where you had hidden the puppy,' Rob's mother said as they walked downstairs.

'So you knew the puppy hadn't died?' Rob asked her.

'You're not very good at telling lies, Rob, I'm glad to say.'

'Then why did you place flowers on the pretend grave?'

'When I heard the Army Procurement Officer quizzing you about the puppy, I thought if there were flowers on the grave and I pointed that out to him, then your story would be more convincing.'

'But you kept doing it,' said Rob.

'It was so that if he returned to check up on us . . . he'd never dream we'd keep putting fresh flowers on a pretend grave.'

'Oh!' Relief surged through Rob. His mum hadn't been so mixed up in her head about things after all. Despite her anxiety and grief, she'd been looking out for him and Millie.

'Did you think I'd gone a bit crazy?'

'Well,' said Rob, 'I knew it must have been you who was putting the flowers there, and I thought maybe' – he paused for a second – 'maybe you believed that Dad had died and had given up hope.'

'It's true I've been very depressed. I should say sorry to you both for putting another burden on your shoulders. It was you, my children, who supported me.'

And she pulled Rob and Millie close, and put her arms around them.

'I wasn't trying to steal your pup.'

Rob glanced up from where he was sitting in the potting shed watching his sister brush Sandy's coat. He saw a different, changed Jed from the one he'd known at school.

'The clinic had borrowed scythes from Farmer Gordon that Sunday morning so that the men could clear the overgrown pathways. I thought I'd better move your puppy at once in case they found him.'

'I'm so glad you did,' said Millie, 'and that you were there when we needed you.'

'And we're glad you came with us when we went to meet the hospital train yesterday,' added Rob.

'Don't know if I liked being kissed by that nurse,' said Jed.

'Nurse Evans was so happy when we told her that Daddy was getting better that she kissed everybody in sight.'

'Even Bert and Chesney,' giggled Millie.

'Let's hope she doesn't try to kiss Captain Morrison when she gives him my thank-you letter,' said Rob.

'I told the engine driver that I'd still bring them plum-jam sandwiches,' said Millie. 'And Mummy is going to bake them some cakes too. They all deserve a present for the help they gave us.'

'Here.' Jed thrust something at her. 'There's a present for you. I'd to tie Sandy to a tree with a bit of string when I came to help carry the stretcher. But a smart dog like that needs a proper collar and lead.'

'Thank you.' Millie opened up the crumpled parcel. 'These are lovely, Jed. Did you make them yourself?'

'It's no bother.' He shrugged. 'Just some leather strips I plaited together.'

'Sandy will be so proud to wear this collar. Look!' Millie showed it to the puppy. 'See what Jed made specially for you?' She slipped the collar around the dog's neck. Then she handed the end of the lead to Jed. 'You can take Sandy for a walk if you like.'

He didn't need a second invitation. Jed grasped the end of the lead and rapidly walked away, as if he thought Millie might change her mind.

'That was a kind thing to do,' Rob said to her.

'I know,' she agreed.

Rob laughed. And as he did so, he suddenly realized that it had been months since he'd laughed out loud at anything. And that made him laugh again.

Millie smiled and took his hand, and the two of them went out along the path to visit their father.

EPILOGUE

Weeks later, when their father was able to be moved downstairs to a bedroom on the first floor, Professor Holt called Rob to the attic room to speak to him.

'I am saying goodbye. This unit has served its purpose, but now the work on blood transfusion is progressing so fast that I am to go elsewhere. We hope to develop a portable machine which will take blood nearer to where the soldiers are fighting. This should save thousands of lives. In time I will return to Belgium. Your determination to find your father has given me hope that I might find my own family.'

The professor handed Rob a box. 'This was found in the eaves of this room. It contains books and toys and games belonging to the boy who once lived in this house. He became a soldier and was killed at the start of the war when he tried and failed to save the life of a fellow soldier. It sounds as if he was a decent sort of man, so I'm sure he wouldn't mind his things being put to good use. Perhaps you'd like to sort them out and leave them in the drawing room. They would serve to amuse any children who come to visit.'

Rob took the box and Professor Holt locked the door behind them.

In the drawing room Rob looked at the toys: a pull-along horse, a wooden fort with soldiers. They were the toys of the little boy who had grown up to become a soldier himself – the man whose spirit had been searching for a soul to save. Rob picked up the books. From between the pages of one, a photograph slid out.

It was a view of the front of Mill House. On the lawn of cropped grass a lady stood holding a croquet mallet in one hand. She'd stopped in the middle of her game to look up at the house. Her other hand was raised to wave. Distinctly in the thirteenth window, waving back at her, Rob saw a figure in white.

After visiting was over, Rob and Nell walked down the driveway with Millie and Sandy. When they reached the main gates, Rob looked round. The sun was casting a dazzling golden light on the front of Mill House.

He stared directly at the top floor. He wasn't at all afraid of what he saw there. Raising his right arm, Rob touched his fingers to his forehead.

From the end attic window the ghost soldier returned the salute.

ABOUT THERESA BRESLIN

THERESA BRESLIN is the Carnegie Medal winning author of over thirty books for children & young adults whose work has appeared on stage, radio and TV. Her books are hugely popular with young people, librarians and teachers. *Remembrance*, her top selling YA novel of youth in WW1, has now been reissued to include Book Notes. *The Dream Master* was shortlisted for the Children's Book Award. *Divided City* was shortlisted for ten book awards, winning two outright.